ALWAYS UNIQUE

ALWAYS UNIQUE

Nikki Turner

ST. MARTIN'S GRIFFIN

New York

ALWAYS UNIQUE. Copyright © 2014 by Nikki Turner.
All rights reserved. Printed in the United States of
America. For information, address St. Martin's Press,
175 Fifth Avenue, New York, N.Y. 10010.

The parts in this book were previously published as
individual e-books.

Unique. Copyright © 2012 by Nikki Turner.

Unique II: Betrayal. Copyright © 2012 by Nikki Turner.

Unique III: Revenge. Copyright © 2012 by Nikki Turner.

www.stmartins.com

The Library of Congress Cataloging-in-Publication Data
is available upon request.

ISBN 978-1-250-04302-3 (trade paperback)
ISBN 978-1-4668-4103-1 (e-book)

St. Martin's Griffin books may be purchased for educational,
business, or promotional use. For information on bulk
purchases, please contact Macmillan Corporate and
Premium Sales Department at 1-800-221-7945, extension
5442, or write specialmarkets@macmillan.com.

First Edition: March 2014

10 9 8 7 6 5 4 3 2 1

This book is dedicated to every girl
who has constantly tried to find herself and
to my very best friend, brother, confidant, and ride or die,
Damien Quarrels.

CONTENTS

ACKNOWLEDGMENTS

I have to thank God, for watching over me and keeping the amazing opportunities pouring in. My Timmond, for being so mature and understanding, you make me so proud of the young man you are turning into in front of my eyes. Continue to reach for your dreams. Determination will get you a long ways! Kennisha, you're such a lady now and I love our relationship. Our candid talks mean everything to me. Stay focused and keep working toward your goals. Malonia, my baby girl, nobody can put a smile on my face and warm my heart like you. Mom, thank you for hanging in there with me. The older I get and the more I learn about life . . . there's a newfound respect for you. Acra, my dad, thanks for stepping up to the plate when I needed you most. That makes up for everything else. My Day One Craig, through it all, you remain the same, and for that I will always love you. Dame, my best friend, thank you for understanding, and always being there. No words can really express my thanks for the way you always show up and show out for me. I'm thankful for you, our friendship, movement, and your encouragement.

Monique P, your patience means the world to me! I know it's been a rough year but you always hung in there with me. And even though I'm sure I've driven you to drink, you faithfully cheered me on! I adore you so much and love you for the way you believe in me and my vision and works. Marc G., for always keeping me with a gig and telling me how it is. Alexandra S., you are the best publishing assistant for sure. You are always on point and on time. Your demeanor and your spirit always make things so easy. To every one of my loyal Nikki Turner readers, none of this would be possible without you! You all continue to push me, inspire me, and support me. Endless thank-yous to you!

UNIQUE

PROLOGUE

It was exactly 12:45 in the afternoon when Unique Bryant entered the Seventh Avenue high-rise. She was focused, and her mind was set on what she had come for, which was nothing short of handling *her* business. Arms folded across her chest and tapping her high-heeled, stiletto Giuseppe Zanotti, "come fuck me" pumps, she waited for the elevator to welcome her through its doors. And just like the last few times that she had been in the lobby of this establishment, she still admired the fact that no expense was spared when the owner commissioned the city's top design firm to furnish the prime, luxury commercial space. A majestic mahogany desk was positioned atop a handmade Persian rug in front of the floor-to-ceiling window that covered the entire east wall. The view of the city was not only spectacular, it was absolutely breathtaking. The other walls were covered with a blond-textured silk fabric and were adorned with expensively framed paintings by artists with names she had never heard of or could barely pronounce.

"Hi, I'm going in," Unique stated with a smile upon exiting the elevator as she made her way past the assistant sitting outside of the executive's office who Unique was going to see. Not waiting for an approval, response, or even taking a second to acknowledge the dirty looks the secretary was giving her, Unique strolled on through like she owned the place. *Let Lil' Kim and Nicki Minaj battle all they want; it's clear, in this moment, who the true Queen Bee really is,* Unique thought as she threw her long hair over her shoulder and kept it moving to the destination at hand.

Unique sashayed into his office with a white and blue bag filled with his favorite brownies from an uptown bakery.

"I thought you had school until six," he asked, happy but puzzled to see her since she wasn't in the culinary classes that he bankrolled.

"They let us out early due to ventilation problems." She dropped the brownies on his desk.

"Did you make these?" He saw the bag from the bakery but he asked the silly question anyway, mesmerized by her complete being. She was wearing a low-cut, short, red Herve Leger dress from which he couldn't peel his eyes away . . . not until she stepped behind his desk, dropped to her knees, and started unbuckling his belt.

"No, I picked them up for you, babe. I figured they were the next best thing to my baking them for you," she answered, as she became preoccupied with his Italian leather belt.

He knew he had a meeting in five minutes, but Unique had the belt undone on his tailored slacks and his dick in her hand before he had a chance to protest— that is, if he had been stupid enough to do something as ridiculous as protest. Even former President Clinton knew better than to exercise his veto power to protest a blow job and Monica Lewinsky's oral game had nothing on Unique's state-of-the-art head jobs. Besides, he'd learned that when it came to Unique's spontaneity, it was always best to let her do her. And the girl did her, oh, so well.

The lucky fellow on the receiving end of Unique's naughty but kind gesture was Kennard DuVall. He was a dapper guy with plenty of that Harlem U.S.A. swagg. He never left the house unless he was suited and booted from head to toe. Indeed, he had the best of both worlds: he was a hugely successful boxing promoter putting together world-class prizefights, and still had a hand and a foot in the know of the streets. But *nothing* was more phenomenal to him than the blows he was getting to the head from Unique. Not only was she drop-dead gorgeous with her exotic looks, but her greatest attribute was that she was a world-class "head boxer" herself.

Unique had her lips around his penis like they were Vise-Grips, and when Kennard was almost at the point where he was about to bust off, his secretary's annoying high-pitched voice distracted him as it came across the intercom.

"Mr. DuVall," she said, "your one P.M. is here."

"Damn!" Kennard responded under his breath. He'd almost forgotten about the appointment just that quickly. But not only that, she fucked up his nut. Surely that was grounds for him to fire the bitch. Regaining his senses, he said, "Okay, tell them to give me ten minutes to finish up here," before stabbing the disconnect button with his finger. "Shit."

Unique's $1,500 hair weave filled his lap. "All I need is two minutes. I promise I got you," she said, never once looking up or losing focus on her task at hand.

Though the sound of her voice made him lose his concentration, it didn't make him lose his hard on, especially with Unique on her job the way she always was. She knew that Kennard was in heaven.

From prior experience, Unique was certain that Kennard's eyes were rolling to the back of his head when she heard the high-pitched moans of pleasure escape his clinched teeth as she submerged one, then the other of his heavy balls into her mouth. A little noon head was her way of saying, *"Hello, honey, how's your day going?"* And if it hadn't already been going good, after this mission Unique was on, it would be guaranteed to be going pretty damn great.

Kennard called out, "Jesus . . . ," and he wasn't even Christian, as Unique executed her patented and creative head-boxing technique with her tongue and jaws.

Bobbing and weaving, then sucking and slurping a few more times, Unique made sure that Kennard was unable to control himself as he busted off in her sexy hot, wet mouth.

Of course, she swallowed every drop of his warm sweet cum, just like it was a Slurpee on a hot summer day.

Then she kissed him on the lips after standing up and straightening out her dress. "What time are you getting out of here tonight?" she asked.

"I got a good mind to leave with you now," he said, tugging at his belt.

"No, don't let me be a distraction," she said with a smile. "Let me get that for you," she purred, helping him with his slacks.

"Believe me, baby, you've done enough. Thank you." He kissed her on her forehead, managing to regain a little of his composure. "I'll ring you at about eight. I got something special planned—if you're not too busy with school stuff or what?"

She was reapplying her "Oh Baby" MAC tinted Lipglass. Then she threw him an air kiss and said, "Stop playing." She used her hazel eyes to do the rest of the talking. "You know I'm never too busy to be with you."

"Then I'll call you."

From his expression, there was no denying that he was pleased. Her eyes beamed at being able to bless him with such a pleasure. She took great pride in getting him off and with Kennard, she couldn't help but feel it was definitely better to give than to receive.

On her way to the elevator, Sandra, the receptionist, had the audacity to roll her eyes at Unique as she strolled past, making it the second time that day in a matter of a five-minute time span she'd caused someone's eyes to roll in the back of their head.

Bitch, fuck you! Unique thought, as she smiled at Sandra and said, "Toodles!" with a wave and kept it moving.

Unique didn't feel one bit of shame. Shit, life was good! She'd come a long way from sucking dicks in the back room of car lots and bathrooms in clubs and especially the whorehouses of Mexico. What in the hell did she care what some receptionist thought about her?

In her lifetime, Unique had slept with a couple of girls in prison and a countless number of guys—*always* for her own manipulative gain—but it was a fact that everyone she laid down with had gotten up and walked away happy campers and had run back and begged for more. But Kennard was different: actually being with someone because she wanted him to have her was a whole other story and definitely a new page in her book of life.

Unique had been through a lot, but she never felt sorry for herself or complained about her plight. Growing up in the unpredictable, violent streets of Richmond, Virginia, taught her to squeeze lemons and make them crystal-clear yellow diamonds. There were people who would label some of her past actions as the epitome of shiesty, raunchy, despicable, and definitely trifling. But Unique would argue that, before Kennard, her life had been about survival of the fittest. Let her tell it, she'd had grown-woman problems and grown-woman bills to pay, which meant she had to do grown-woman things. Regardless of what it was called these days, though, Unique had indeed been through enough madness and drama to fill an epic motion picture and a few blockbuster sequels. So pleasing a guy who was not only rich but who was crazy about her—and she actually felt the same for him—made her feel like she had hit the Lotto. She never thought the day would come when *she* was the one falling in love—and the irony: his money didn't matter to her. Now, make no mistake about it—she was happy Kennard had money, but if he didn't come to the table with as much, she would have felt the same way about him. She was a hustler and without a doubt, by hook or by crook, if she knew nothing else, she knew how to get money.

Fuck scratching off a lottery ticket or going on a trip to Vegas in the hopes of winning big—Unique had been born with the jackpot right between her legs and a bonus on her tongue. But Kennard had it all: money, a big dick (and he knew what to do with it), swagger, a lucrative company, and so much love for her that in her eyes, life was good.

Unique was certain that her old ways weren't the life she wanted for herself anymore. Kennard cared for her and admired her so much that she wanted to turn over a new leaf for him and to be all the woman he needed her to be. He was her new beginning and her road to riches and happiness. Her two-bit hustles were finally a thing of her past.

In her previous life, a treacherous guy named Lootchee had bought out her contract from the Mexican whorehouse and brought her back to Virginia, only to hold it over her head and treat her like a slave. After she escaped that situation, she started to reflect on her life and couldn't get a wink of sleep as she thought about all the shameful deeds she had done in that city. Her friend, Tyeedah, whom she met in prison, convinced her to come to New York about a year ago. It didn't take much persuading. Unique quickly got on the first thing smoking to New York City with only four hundred dollars and a suitcase full of skeletons. She had no real plan, and the big city and big lights were the only things on her mind. Back home, her pastor and his wife told her that the city would eat her alive. But she knew firsthand that what didn't kill her only would make her stronger. Besides, what more damage could this city do to her that hadn't already been done? After all, she was the same girl who had survived after being abandoned in Mexico, with no passport, by the only man she ever really loved; where she was forced to buy back her freedom by selling her body to dirty-dick, drunk, uncircumcised Mexicans.

If she wanted to be a boxer in her arena, she damn sure couldn't have a glass chin. So Unique took it like the champ she was. After all, she was used to swimming in deep waters with the sharks, so she came to the city of dreams ready to take her bite out of the Big

Apple, fully expecting a rocky ride. But instead, she found that life in the city was nothing but smooth sailing, especially after she happened to be in the right place at the right time. She had only been in New York for less than two weeks when she bumped into Kennard—literally. They collided in a crowded room. He accidentally spilled his drink on her, and since then they were in a whirlwind tango.

Unique strutted out the building like a runway model to her Mercedes-Benz S500, which Kennard had been paying for during the past nine months that they had been together. Funny thing was, she drove his Maserati more than she drove her own car. She loved everything about it. But the truth of the matter was it could have been an orange Oldsmobile Delta 88, and she would have driven that with great poise and pride. Hell, even after Cinderella's carriage turned into a pumpkin, at the end of the story, the chick was still a princess. The mere fact that Kennard released his car to her with no hesitation made her feel that she was something special to him. God was indeed good, she thought as she looked in the visor mirror to check her makeup. Talk about bringing her through the storm.

Once she pulled out of her parking space, she noticed a promotional flyer under the windshield wiper of the car. The bright orange paper started to annoy her so she pulled over to remove it. She got partially out of the car to reach for the piece of paper. Once she set her perfectly round butt back in the bucket seat, she realized that it wasn't a flyer that some promoter's street team had left on the window of a row of cars. It was a personal note. She opened it up and read: WHER-EVER YOU GO . . . THERE YOU ARE!

Unique looked around; though she was pretty positive it had to be a mix-up, it puzzled the shit out of her. Was this meant for her? It couldn't have been. She was still so new to the city, and she had been flying deep below the radar. She hadn't made any enemies or showed any traits from her old life. Her entire focus these days was culinary school and keeping Kennard happy. She wanted so much for him to make their relationship official. She was well aware that his kind wasn't accustomed to making hoes into housewives, but she was hopeful that the hoe-God would work things out in her favor.

The letter was baffling to Unique. Maybe it was meant for Kennard. After all, he drove her car occasionally and he had a lot of enemies. Kennard had done a lot for the people in his Harlem hood. He was respected by many but feared by just as much. He had been a street dude and lived by the sword. He'd also had a lot of money deals, and while most were lovely, some were mediocre, and a few went sour. Yes, this letter could very well be meant for Kennard.

Whatever the meaning was between the lines of that letter, Unique didn't want any problems. But from past experience, whether Unique wanted problems or not, they always seem to attach themselves to her.

THE FOOT DRAGON

Unique tried not to rack her brain to figure out the why, where, and who of the mysterious note. She hadn't the foggiest idea who had put it there or why. Besides Kennard, she barely knew anyone in New York. As big as the apple was, why in the hell did someone have to try to take a bite out of her?

After thinking long and hard, Unique could only come up with a few logical explanations for the letter.

Could someone have mistaken my car for someone else's? I mean, there are a bunch of Mercedes driving around New York City. Maybe the note could be meant for Kennard? He does drive this car a lot. And, I know his business tactics are mostly on the up-and-up, but nevertheless, just like me, he's had his share of the streets some years ago. Or, wait a minute! What the hell am I thinking? It could be one of Kennard's ex-bitches trying to start some shit. I wish a bitch would try to come between me and Kennard. These NY chicks don't want to get me started! They don't know me and got me fucked up! Sorry bitches—you snooze, you lose. Your loss, my gain. Bitches kill me . . . old news, I'm the new news! Fuck outta here!

Unique was getting too worked up about the letter. To keep herself from going crazy, she made a conscious decision to not let it rent any more room in her head. She had too many positive things going on.

Since she had the day off from school, she decided to spend the afternoon hunting for the perfect pair of shoes to go with a teal dress that she'd bought last week. Saks Fifth Avenue, Bergdorf Goodman, and a couple of boutiques later, she fell in love with a pair of must-have Christian Louboutin designs. Three shoe-gasms later, and a visit to the spa for her biweekly wax as well as a hot stone massage to relax her muscles. She knew that later that night at home, she was destined to finish what she started at Kennard's office. It was close to 8 P.M.—7:59 to be exact—when she was done, and just like clockwork, her phone rang.

Good-looking, rich, and punctual, she thought. *How often does a man like that come along? And how lucky can one girl be?*

"Hello, my love!" she answered, with all smiles.

"Excuse me, I must have the wrong number."

"Oh, you got jokes?" she said. Even if the caller ID hadn't done its job, Unique would have known Kennard's brisk, sexy, thick New York accent anywhere.

"I hope you're on the way to Jersey now, making your way home."

Unique checked the side mirror and then changed lanes. "Twenty minutes. I'm in the car now."

"Good," he said.

"That's it? Only good? I got a better welcome by the waiter at lunch," she teased.

"Now you're the one with jokes." If there was one chink in Kennard's confident exterior, it was his jealous streak. "We missed the ESPN piece. It aired late last night. I've been getting calls about it all day."

ESPN conducted an in-depth interview with Kennard, focusing on his success in and out of work. It was filmed at three locations: his office, his boxing gym, and his home in Englewood Cliffs, New Jersey, where lighting had been set up in the great room that showcased his opulent furniture and lifestyle.

During the interview, the reporter asked what Kennard did in his spare time, and without hesitation, he said, "I try to spend as much of it as possible with this lady here." The cameraman got a close-up of Unique, who was sitting off to the side, admiring her man. Kennard continued, "We enjoy our life together and the fruits of my hard work."

"OMG! OMG! OMG! Babe, that's so great!" Unique knew how much he'd been looking forward to it. "How come no one told you when it was airing? That's crazy that we missed it, but even crazier that we didn't even know it was coming on."

"They put it on a few days earlier than planned. One of the producers at the network tried to contact me but he couldn't get through."

"And he didn't leave a message?"

"Actually, he did try," Kennard said sheepishly, "but you know"—he paused—"my voice mailbox was full."

Unique had chastised Kennard for months about clearing out his voice mail. "Kennard . . ."

"I know," he said, before she could beat him up about it. "I need a better assistant."

That wasn't what she was thinking at all. His assistant, Roger, couldn't reach him half the time and neither could the receptionist, Sandra. But she knew how busy Kennard was. In all actuality, even though Unique knew that Sandra wasn't in her fan club, she still felt sorry for the woman because Kennard not only did exactly what he wanted to do but he was all over the place. Her job was impossible, and the poor woman was always busy, but she would have to admit he juggled everything the best he could.

"You know how it is, though," Kennard continued. "If you want something done right, you have to do it yourself. That's why I made a promise to myself to clean out my messages every day from now on."

"Sounds like a great idea," she said sarcastically. "An idea that I've been trying to make a reality for like nine months now."

"I'm full of good ideas, baby. That's why I'm with you."

"That's not all you are full of, either," she said.

"You're making reference to the bulge in my pockets or the one in my pants?" he teased.

"Neither."

"What?" He sounded shocked and offended.

"Okay. You're definitely packing where it counts, but . . ."

There was a *click* on the line; someone else was trying to get through to him.

"I hafta take this call, babe. See you when you get here. Love you."

"Love you, too."

After hanging up, Unique turned the music up. The words "I love you" soothed every muscle in her body. Her jam, "Motivation," was on the radio and she began singing out loud. She'd butchered the first three verses of Kelly Rowland's song when she noticed a car behind hers. It was a dark-colored, late-model Honda. And now that she thought about it, she was almost certain that she had seen that same car when she left the spa.

Unique eased her foot off the accelerator, giving the car the opportunity to go around her, but it didn't pass. The driver of the Honda also slowed down, scaling back at least two car lengths behind.

She gazed into the mirror. *What the hell? I know this car ain't following me!* Still, she thought about the letter and decided that it might be smart to take precautions in case they were related.

Unique was nearly home. She could keep driving, but if someone was following her, she didn't want to lead them to where she and Kennard laid their heads. Kennard always warned her to be vigilant of the stickup and carjack mob. Because she was from the South, Kennard—like most New Yorkers—thought that meant she was a little naïve. And like most New Yorkers, he definitely let the area code, the zip code, and the accent fool him, because when it came to Unique, he couldn't have been more wrong. Unique had definitely been around the block a few times and knew more than what Kennard credited her for.

Unique was trying to figure out what she was going to do, when it hit her that there was a large grocery store about two miles ahead on the right. The parking lot was well lit and normally filled with customers coming and going. If the Honda was still behind her when she reached the store, she decided she would turn in and see what would happen from there. *Only a fool or*

*a bold bastard would try something stupid in a brightly lit
area in front of a bunch of witnesses.*

Two miles later, she glanced in the mirror and the
Honda was still there. *Ain't this a beyatch!*

Unique hit her turn signal and busted a right into
the parking lot. Navigating the Benz through the well-
populated area, she didn't stop until she was in front of
the store.

The driver of the Honda came right in behind her.
Unless the driver coincidently needed to stop for bread,
milk, and eggs, it was now official that the Honda was
following her.

And for the first time tonight, Unique started to
get a little nervous when the fool drove past, turned
around, and then parked directly behind her. She tried
to get a look at the driver but the windows on the
Honda were tinted.

Unique sat there in the busy parking lot, watching
the Honda and then watching the clock as seconds
turned into minutes. The Honda hadn't budged. There
was a Mexican standoff going on between her and the
driver of the Honda.

Unique was getting pissed. *Fuck this shit. First the
letter, now this shit.* Emboldened by the lights and crowd,
Unique stepped out of her car. She was done with the
games.

She knew now that it probably wasn't a carjack

mob or any stickup kids because if it was, they would already have been over at her car, pulling her out or putting her in the trunk of the Honda.

This shit is crazy!

Unique thought she had it figured it out: *It had to be one of Kennard's old foot dragons.* That's what she called a jilted lover or a bed warmer who didn't know how to accept rejection. A clinger. When the person hears it's over, he or she drops to their knees and grabs you by the foot, begging you not to leave as their pathetic asses are dragged across the floor. Unique knew better than to let her emotions override her intellect and she was more of a lover than a fighter, but this scenario was getting out of control. She felt that she had to take matters in her own hands and had no choice but to straighten out the low-self-esteem bitch and then go home to her man. This broad was becoming a major distraction and a waste of time.

I have to nip this nonsense in the bud! she told herself when she opened up the door and stomped her way toward the Honda, prepared to kick a little ass if she had to, heels or no heels. She was halfway to the car, close enough to hear the engine idling. Then it struck her that the engine was idling too loud, and she saw the car jerk a bit as if the driver was putting it in gear. But before her body could react to what her ears were hearing, her eyes were seeing the tires spinning out before the Honda lurched forward.

Unique wanted to stand firm so she could come eye to eye with this dragon, but she was no fool; she needed to haul it back to her car because the chicken head was trying to run her over. Or scare the living life out of her.

While she was momentarily frozen, she had good reflexes. Her stilettos were in the asphalt like a carpenter's nail in a piece of plywood but this was no horror movie; she took off like a track star and ran to her car.

Unique wasn't about to get run over by a raggedy Honda in the middle of a supermarket parking lot. She could feel the heat coming from the engine as it got closer. Inches before colliding with her, it swerved, barely missing her.

"Bitch ass!" she said out loud, no longer nervous. Now she was just flat-out mad. Unique ran back to the Benz, jumped behind the wheel, and took off after the runaway Honda.

She caught up easily. *Motherfucking bitches wanna follow me, I'm going to show this motherfucker about fucking with me.*

Unique was on the Honda's bumper, where the license plate was conveniently concealed behind a patch of mud. The driver got the message and knew Unique wasn't to be fucked with. The Honda made it known that it wanted out of this cat-and-mouse game, mashing the pedal to the metal, but it was no competition for Unique and her V12 engine. Unique was right on the Honda's bumper, and she was thinking about ramming the Honda in the rear end. She knew she had the Honda exactly where she wanted it and could make it stop.

But enough was enough. She had somewhere she needed to be. As she contemplated bringing this whole mess to an end with an accident, she hesitated too long, giving the driver a chance to veer onto the George Washington Bridge. Unique screamed at the Honda as if it could hear her, "That's right, keep booking, be-yatch!!!!"

LOVING BEING LOVED

On her way home Unique was trying to decide what she should tell Kennard. She wanted to tell him to get his exes in check. Still, hindsight being twenty-twenty, she was embarrassed by the way she had acted and wondered what Kennard would think of her. But all of her thoughts went out the window once she put her key in the door and stepped into the house.

She could not believe her eyes: Kennard had gone all out for her.

The lighting was dimmed to a seductive low. And flickering candles provided just enough illumination to make out the trail of rose petals he'd left for her to follow.

"Kennard," she called out sexily.

When he didn't answer, she kicked off her heels and followed the white rose petals. The floral path continued through the foyer, through the great room, up the spiral staircase, down the Australian hardwood hallway, and into the master bedroom.

There she found more candles, and rose petals on the bed in the shape of a big heart. There were hundreds of petals of various colors: red, white, yellow, and pink.

"Material Things" by Avant flowed from the custom speakers that were built into the walls. Kennard still hadn't revealed himself, but his presence was definitely felt all through the house. As she looked around, Unique couldn't help but think that if she lost all of this, one day she might be a mad bitch in a Honda, too.

"I hope the reason you're taking so long to get here is because you are getting undressed," Kennard said from the bathroom.

Unique's nipples perked up at the sound of his voice. Her vagina had been wet since she stepped into the house and smelled those scented candles.

"I'm going to let you undress me," she said as she stepped into the spa-sized bathroom. "If that's okay with you?"

Kennard had continued the rose theme in the sunken Jacuzzi. He sat in one of the dressing chairs, wearing nothing but black silk pajama bottoms and a seductive smile. His body was hard and chiseled like a Greek statue. "Your wish is my command, my queen. You merely have to say it, and it shall be granted."

"Then what you waiting for?" Unique was ready to

get this party started. "Come, daddy, and undress your queen."

Kennard did exactly what his woman asked. He methodically removed one piece of clothing at a time: dress, then panties, then bra. It was like peeling a banana. He paid extra attention to the *soft spots.*

Unique's body was on fire by the time her designer clothes hit the marble floor, and she was ready to be extinguished. As if he could read her mind, Kennard stepped out of his bottoms and scooped her up off of her feet and carried her to the Jacuzzi, which was big enough to hold eight people. The rose petals parted as he submerged her naked body into the perfectly heated water and the scent of lavender wafted through the air.

They made slow, jet-powered aquatic love for the next hour, but the real sex took place above water, in their bed. Kennard had thought of everything. They got freaky with the *Kama Sutra,* along with oils, chocolates, fruits, and whipped cream as an appetizer. The night progressed like a hedonistic holiday. It was Independence Day, and the fireworks didn't stop exploding until deep into the wee hours of the morning. Afterward, they fell asleep and spent the night in each other's arms.

When the alarm on Kennard's phone sounded and nudged them awake at exactly 8:00 A.M., he hit the snooze button. They spooned for the next fifteen minutes on crumpled rose petals until the pushy alarm went off again.

"Babe, we need to get up," Kennard said.

Unique pouted. "Don't we have time for a quickie?" She wanted him to think of nothing but her while he was at work.

Kennard looked at the time, then reluctantly pulled himself from the bed. He playfully whacked her on the butt. "How about you give me a rain check?" he said. "I have to wash this chocolate out of my ears before I go to work." His semi-hard manhood had a mind of its own, however, and it seemed to like Unique's idea better.

"You weren't complaining about how sticky you were last night," she said playfully.

"That's because last night I was putting in work."

"And you definitely were, babe," she agreed. "I tell you what . . . if you come back to bed right now, to save you some time, I'll lick the chocolate off of every part of your body and clean you up real good, baby," she offered in her sexiest voice.

She wiped her tongue across her lips to show him what he would be missing in case he'd forgotten.

While Kennard thought about the proposition his dick bobbed its head, as if it wanted to say, *Can I get some action?* He didn't think about it for long before jumping back into the bed.

"You're incorrigible," he said.

She eyed his fully erect manhood and then gave him a devilish look. "You're the one holding the gun, not me."

"I beg to differ since you're the one who is about to blow my brains out."

Kennard started kissing her Australian-style—*down under*—and didn't come up for air until she shook. Unique gratefully returned the favor. Afterward, Unique slipped on her thigh-length Agent Provocateur robe and went downstairs to fix Kennard breakfast while he showered.

She whipped up turkey bacon, scrambled eggs, and cheese, and was making sandwiches on toasted croissants when she heard Kennard calling her.

"I'm in the kitchen, babe," she yelled back.

"Damn, something smells good in here," he announced a second later, coming up behind her. He wrapped his hands around Unique's waist, kissing her on the back of the neck. She loved his touch and the chemistry they shared.

Unique turned around and got a look at him. "Dayum!"

Kennard wore a brand-new tailored, Italian-cut suit, light gray with a four-button jacket; a crisp, striped, buttoned-up gray, black, and white shirt; and black leather Gucci loafers. "Somebody's looking good this morning!" she said.

Kennard struck one of his patented magazine poses. "That's where you're wrong, baby."

"Am I?" she said, handing him a plate full of food. "Here, babe."

"Yes, you are." He took a bite of his sandwich. "Because . . . ," he said, with his mouth full, "I look good every morning."

Unique laughed. "And that you do. I'd be the first to second that." She tried to give him a playful love tap on the chest. "But your butt is way too conceited."

"Try confident," he said, brushing off the love tap.

"Try narcissistic," she came back, with a bigger smile.

"Whatever," he said, ending the debate. "You know you love it, though."

"Now, that's true," she confessed. "But that's only because I love everything about you. Even your snoring."

"I only snore when I go to sleep on a full stomach," said Kennard defensively.

She gave him a tell-it-to-somebody-that-don't-sleep-with-you look.

"Okay, so I snore," he admitted. "Now, are you going to walk me to the door or are you going to continue to beat me up about the few faults that I may or may not have?"

"Baby, whatever your faults are, I love you all the same, so you're perfect in my eyes."

"You giving me those sweet nothings already and it ain't ten A.M. yet," he said.

"Yeah, your rewards for rising and shining early. You know what they say, the early bird gets the worm." With a sexy smile, Unique walked up and cupped his package.

"And that's exactly why I need to head out. I'm already late."

"Oh, don't you worry about that because the early bird might get the worm, but the second mouse gets the cheese."

"You have way too much wisdom for your own good," he teased. He took one last bite of the sandwich and left the remaining half of the sandwich on the plate on the table. He rose from his chair and hugged her. "Thank you for breakfast."

"Anytime, baby." She smiled.

"I gotta go get the bacon," he said as he kissed her on the forehead and slowly let her go. Then he grabbed his briefcase, and headed for the door. Like a little puppy dog, she followed closely behind him.

Before he left the house, they kissed in the foyer. It was a long, passionate kiss. Unique stood in the doorway until Kennard got into his car and his Maserati had disappeared completely from her sight.

Unique closed the door with a content smile on her lips. It was funny how her life had changed in just under a year. Her life had become a real-life motion picture, and as she stood in the foyer looking around her home, she exhaled in wonderment. Marble floors, granite countertops, vaulted ceilings, a theater room, and a Jacuzzi tub. She couldn't believe this was all hers. Well, half hers. The craziest thing of all was that she was actually in love and hadn't even been looking for it.

A part of her was waiting for the credits to roll, the lights to come up, and to find that she was still in that small bedroom in her grandmother's house in Virginia. But the truth of the matter was that the curtains weren't ready to drop because this drama was hardly at the end.

In fact it was about to get real interesting. . . .

FROM WHORE TO HOUSEWIFE

Unique was still floating on Cloud Love as she walked back into the kitchen to wash the breakfast dishes but as she was about to enter the room, she got stopped in her tracks.

"I thought I would never find your sneaky ass," a voice said. "I bet you didn't think I would, either, huh?"

Startled, Unique's head jerked toward the voice, and when she looked, she couldn't believe her eyes when she saw who was sitting at her kitchen table, eating the rest of the sandwich that Kennard had left behind.

The man was slim and dark-skinned with a big nose and mean eyes. She'd never seen him before. Her first instinct was to run; her second instinct was to pick up something to defend herself. He saw her eyeing the butcher knives on the counter but her hands were not as fast as her thoughts were. She was reaching for the knife when he whipped out a big 9mm.

"Don't even think about it, *Unique*," he warned, his voice firm and intimidating. He said her name as if it were a deadly cancer. The gun was trained steadily on her. In return, she looked at him as if he not only smelled like shit but he *was* shit. This man had the nerve to come in her house and sit at her table and talk smack to her? What part of the game was this?

But the warning wasn't needed. Unique knew better than to bring a knife to a gunfight. As she stood there eyeing his gun, he let out a chuckle.

"You don't even remember me, do you?" Then he smiled at her with a mouth filled with silver teeth.

That's when it hit her like a freight train. She'd know that yuck mouth anywhere.

"Fat Tee," she said, nodding. "Definitely a blast from the past." She knew him from her days in Richmond, Virginia, only he wasn't fat anymore. All the weight he had lost, and the fact that his face looked like all the life had been sucked out of it, made it almost impossible for her to recognize him on sight.

"And what the hell are you doing in my house?" Unique knew that he wasn't there to catch up on old times. The last time she had seen him, it hadn't ended on good terms. She had pretended that she liked him so that Took, her boyfriend at the time, could rob him blind. He should've known better. Why would he even believe that a chick as fine as her would look his way other than for monetary gain? There was no denying that Fat Tee was getting money back then and had the whole neighborhood on lock, but judging how he was looking now, it seemed that things had slackened off a little for him.

Fat Tee had been an obnoxious oaf, but he had proved to be an easy victim for Unique during her guttersnipe days. After gaining his trust, Fat Tee kept no secrets, including where he kept all his money and drugs. That's when Unique persuaded him to take her to Atlantic City while Took and a couple of friends dressed as movers and cleaned out his house. They stole a half million dollars in drugs and cash, and didn't stop there. They stole all his furniture and even took the food out of the man's refrigerator. The sting went off so sweet that Fat Tee's neighbors even aided them; they didn't care for him much anyway and were ecstatic at the thought of him moving. Happy to be getting rid of him, they actually served "the movers" lemonade to help fight off the heat.

When Unique and Fat Tee got back from Atlantic City, she didn't even go back to Fat Tee's house with him. She made up a b.s. excuse about how she needed to stop by a girlfriend's place. Being the doting boyfriend, Fat Tee obliged. He dropped her off and told her he would see her later. Well, later was seven years ago.

"I've been looking for you for a real long time. Heard you had made your way to the Big Apple—big city, big dreams." He drank the rest of the orange juice out of the carton that had been left on the table. He belched. "I'd been in this overcrowded city searching for you for over three months now on a one-bug scavenger hunt, from hood to project, from project to strip club, and then I hit up the record labels."

Unique didn't say anything. Two things ran through her mind: first, she hoped that Kennard hadn't left anything behind, causing him to double back and walk through that door; second, how in the hell was she going to get this loser out of her damn house?

He smiled. "And just when I was about to give up, I saw you on ESPN. Fucking ESPN. Who'd have thought? I was shocked, but I ain't surprised. After I saw you and your boy, I Googled him, got his work address, and then waited outside his office for three hours until you pulled up in your brand-new Benz."

Unique crossed her arms and looked him dead in the eyes. "Cut the bullshit background story. What do you want, Fat Tee?" She wasn't going to let him intimidate her.

He looked at her like she was the old Unique, like she was still a bag of trash in his eyes. Unique tightened the belt on her robe, wishing she had something on that was a little less revealing.

"I want a million dollars. That's what I want. A million fucking dollars, bitch!"

She looked at him as if he had lost his mind. "A million fucking dollars?" She repeated it, then cackled as if it was the funniest thing she had ever heard.

"This ain't no joke, or no laughing matter, Unique."

"Fat Tee, seriously, like where in the hell am I going to get a million dollars?" she asked, as if he knew something that she didn't.

"Being that you are such a scheming, conniving, clever thieving bitch, you figure that shit out." Those words hurt Unique not because they came from him, but because the truth hurt. His words reminded her of who she used to be and all the memories she was trying to forget.

"Steal it from this motherfucker." He pointed to a picture of Kennard that was hanging on the wall. "Or the gotdamn Easter Bunny for all I care. I could give a fuck. Just get it."

Kennard knew almost nothing about her past. He knew she was from Virginia but had said that he was more concerned about what they could do together in the future, rather than what they'd done with other people in the past.

Unique was nobody's fool. She knew that was Kennard's way of avoiding talking about all those skank bitches who were always smiling up in his face. But Unique had rolled with his philosophy because she had her own skeletons. Now one of those skeletons was sitting in their kitchen, asking for a million dollars.

Unique looked directly into Fat Tee's eyes. "You and the Easter Bunny can go suck on an egg," she said derisively. "And I would appreciate it if you would get the fuck out of my house. There's the door." She pointed.

Fat Tee got up, walked over to her, and then smacked her so viciously that she fell to the floor. "Bitch, you don't show me no motherfucking door."

She was on the floor and reaching for something to throw but he was standing over her in such a way that she couldn't move.

"This ain't no motherfucking joke, bitch!" He bent down so that they were eye to eye. "But I can show you better than I can tell you." He smacked her again and then tore her robe open.

Unique yelled, "Get the fuck off of me!" Desperate, she tried to kick him in the nuts. The kick only grazed him, and didn't slow him down at all.

In response, Fat Tee tried to take her head off with a hard-pimp, backhand smack. Then he hit her again. The second blow rattled her brain so hard, Unique almost faded to black. He pushed his body between her legs. She tried to fight him but there was no use—he was much stronger than her.

This bastard is really going to rape me!

He was choking her with one hand while he used

the other to undo his pants. When she tried to move, he applied pressure, cutting off her air even more.

He smiled as he forced himself into her. It was a soulless smirk that grew every time he plunged inside. Unique glared up at him, with tears in her eyes. She wanted nothing more than to kill him for what he was doing to her, but she was defenseless. He was bigger. He was stronger. And he had the upper hand.

She could still smell Kennard's scent on her body from the beautiful love they'd made together as Fat Tee violated her.

When he saw tears roll down her cheeks, it made him more aggressive. He made an ugly face when he came inside of her, uglier than he already was. Even though the tiny-dick bastard finished quickly, the whole scenario seemed to be playing out in slow motion. Every second seemed like an hour.

Unique almost gagged when she thought about this low-down dirty troll's semen mixing with Kennard's, like some vile, disgusting soup congealing in a pot. She thought about the man she loved with all her heart.

She cried.

During all the things she had been through— serving time in a federal prison for crimes that she had not committed, working in the Mexican whorehouse, the lies, the betrayals—Unique had never cried. She always found a way to get even.

"See, I knew some things never change. Same old Unique . . ."—he leaned in with an evil grin—"with the bomb-ass pussy." A wicked laugh escaped his lips.

Unique was boiling with anger as tears continued to stream down her face.

"I don't give a fuck about no tears," Fat Tee said as he stood up and fixed his pants. "That there pussy of yours was the first interest payment on my million fucking dollars. The interest stops when I get all of my money. You heard me?"

Unique looked at him in total disgust, and when she didn't answer, he kicked her in the stomach. It knocked the wind out of her . . . what was left of it anyway.

Fat Tee grabbed an apple off the counter and looked over his shoulder at her lying on the floor, balled up in the fetal position.

As he left, he said, "A million fucking dollars, bitch!"

GET HIM BEFORE HE GETS YOU

Unique took the longest shower of her life. No matter how much she soaped and scrubbed her body, she couldn't get Fat Tee's nasty, disgusting stench off her.

It had taken less than five minutes for Fat Tee to turn the fairy tale she'd been living into a nightmare. Unique just wanted to go back to sleep, and when she woke up, for everything to be like it was. But this wasn't a movie: this was her life and that was one wish that wouldn't be granted.

How can I make this go away? she kept asking herself over and over again.

Her first thought was to flip the script and do what she had been bred to do. Be the hunter instead of the hunted. How hard would it be for her to get her hands on a gun? Not hard at all, she thought. She'd never killed anyone before, but an ex-boyfriend once told her that killing someone wasn't difficult. Living with the knowledge that you've taken another person's life, he had said, was the most difficult part but the actual act gave you an adrenaline rush. The old Unique wouldn't have had any problem whatsoever with knowing that she'd put herself out of the misery and had rid the world of Fat Tee's low-life ass. But she was neither the same girl she used to be nor did she have any desire to be.

So, what were her other options? She couldn't tell Kennard how her jacked-up past had caught up with her. What would she say?

Hey, honey. I know you said that you didn't want to talk about our pasts, but I have one little bitty thing to share with you. It's really no big deal at all. It's just that back in the day, I used to set niggas up to get robbed, that's all. I know how it sounds, but it wasn't really like that. They weren't like you; they deserved it. . . . Trust me, this is as hard for me to say as it is for you to hear, but I have to tell you this. There was this one dude that I lived with for one week. Yeah, that's how long it took for me to rock him to sleep with the pussy. After he broke down and came up off of the combination to his safe and a few other secrets, I passed the information to my boyfriend and gave him the keys to the dude's house. He stole everything the dude had to his name: drugs, money, furniture, everything. Now the dude has surfaced and wants to collect. He wants a million dollars.

Not an option *at all!* She wasn't trying to send

Kennard running, full speed, in the other direction, but she had to come up with something.

After it seemed like her skin was washed raw, she finally abandoned the shower. She examined her entire body in the mirror, and was glad to not find any telltale bruises on her body or face. She exhaled as her cell phone rang while she was toweling off. It was the administration department of the culinary school. Fortunately for her, the ventilation system was still screwed up, and class would most likely be canceled all week. "We will notify you when the problem is corrected or if we relocate the classes," said the woman on the other end of the phone.

Puh-leeze. Lady, you even seen real problems? she thought to herself after thanking the woman for the information and disconnecting the call.

At least she didn't have to go to school and, sitting around a bunch of strangers, feel like a victim. That wasn't what she needed, not this day anyway. What she did need was someone she could confide in, someone that would understand and be nonjudgmental.

There was only one person in New York who fit that criteria.

Tyeedah and Unique had met in the prison camp at Alderson, West Virginia, the same place where Martha Stewart had served her time for insider trading.

Unique and Tyeedah had worked out together. No one could keep up with either of the girls' endurance. In the beginning they didn't talk much. But after months of grueling calisthenics, light weights, and running around the track, they opened up to each other, finding out that they had more in common than just a passion for toning their bodies. Tyeedah knew a lot about Unique and had seen her scheming ways in prison and accepted her for who she was. The friendship forged by Tyeedah and Unique in prison was stronger than two people just trying to pass idle time. They really rode for each other, and the friendship transcended the prison walls.

After a quick phone conversation touching on the basics, Tyeedah told Unique to get her ass to her house. Unique followed her friend's instructions and got dressed and drove to Brooklyn, knowing this wasn't going to be a pity party. She confided in Tyeedah not because she wanted a shoulder to cry on, or needed an ear to listen, but because she knew that, if push came to shove, whatever solution she came up with, the odds were that Tyeedah would be her co-conspirator to help her carry it out.

"I can't believe this shit," Tyeedah said, after hearing the entire story. "For a whole lot less than a million dollars, I can have that clown merked. Deese folks that I'll get to take care of it would make that shit look like an accident." It sounded like some Lifetime Channel drama, but Unique knew one thing for certain: her friend was dead-ass serious.

"I don't want to kill anyone," Unique said firmly. "That's not the route I want to take." Unique had done a lot of foul things in her life. Her actions might have ultimately even caused the death of people, but she wanted to always be able to keep her conscience clear of never being the person behind the trigger.

Tyeedah looked confused. The Unique that she knew had more heart and bigger balls than the above average dude. She was *unsure* about this girl sitting on her couch. It looked like Unique, walked like Unique, but wasn't sounding like the Unique that she had grown to know and love.

"Then where are you going to get a million from without asking or telling Kennard? Even then, is he going to give you that type of cash to hand over to some nigga? Bitch, please." She looked her friend up and down. "I know your shit might be golden, but this sounds like a job for Robert Redford and an indecent proposal," she said. "I know I don't have to remind you that this shit is serious, do I? Fuck. The bastard raped you, Unique. Hellooo! Where is the Unique I did hard time with? The one who didn't give two fucks in a bucket about a nigga or the rachet-ass existence he calls a life."

Unique thought hard and long about what her friend had said before answering. "I don't wanna be her anymore. She was bad news. Big-time. To be honest . . . ," she tried to explain, "Fat Tee is only having a *reaction* to an action I had already put in motion. If I hadn't set him up in the first place, he wouldn't have the need to seek retribution or compensation. It's not like I'm an innocent victim in all this. The shit's like a merry-go-round."

"Okay . . . fine. If you want to be this 'new and improved' person, I support you one hundred percent. But"—Tyeedah paused for emphasis—"first you're going to have to get rid of the skeletons that belong to the *old* you, which could possibly tear down the *new* you."

Tyeedah let her words marinate for a second. Unique took a heavy, restorative breath.

"I know you're feeling Kennard and don't want to fuck up what y'all got. I get that, but you have to handle this nigga, Fat Tee, before you end up with *nothing*. Maybe, not even your life," Tyeedah spat. "Who says he'll stop at a million dollars?"

Everything Tyeedah said was the truth. Unique knew this. But where would it end?

Unique asked, "And how do I deal with the next nigga that finds me? Every nigga Took and I robbed probably saw my face on that show, so tell me how does this all end? Like I said before, it's like a merry-go-round. And where it stops, nobody really knows." After a few moments of silence, she wondered, "Maybe if I can give Fat Tee something to hold him, he'll back off until I can come up with a better solution."

"Fuck that!" Tyeedah said emphatically. "You pay one time, and then you gotta keep paying. That's the way it is for people like him."

"So you're saying, short of killing the dude, there's no way to make this right?"

"Girl, you don't owe him shit. I dig all that action and reaction stuff. And if you really believe that," she said, "then when you and Took robbed Fat Tee, that was a reaction to what he had done, right?" Unique had told Tyeedah that Fat Tee was getting drugs from Took, but when Took got locked up, Fat Tee reneged on what was owed him and gave Unique the runaround when it was time to pay up.

As crazy as it sounded, what Tyeedah was saying had merit.

Unique shook her head. "But I didn't know Took was going to take everything from the man."

Tyeedah wasn't finished putting on her case. "But don't act like the bastard didn't deserve it. From what you told me, the fool showed his entire black ass when Took went to jail. So, didn't Took have a right, according to your action and reaction philosophy, to get what was his, plus a little interest? The way I see it, his bitch ass is just crying over spilled milk after stealing the damn cow."

Unique was starting to feel all of that eye-for-an-eye stuff Tyeedah was talking. But she couldn't help but think that with her and Fat Tee, it was now about to be a silver motherfucking tooth-for-a-tooth.

"So what do you suggest I do?" Unique said, resigned and frustrated.

"I say, merk him or tell him it's a part of the game. And he better hide under a rock in Virginia and pray that you don't get the urge to get loose lips and tell Kennard what he did." Tyeedah realized that she had never seen Unique this indecisive or vulnerable. Her normal take-charge attitude was frayed. The magnitude of the situation and all that was at stake clearly had her friend shaken.

"To be honest," Tyeedah said, "I don't know what you should do. But the bottom line is, whatever you decide, know I got your back."

"Thanks, girl." As Tyeedah gave her a reassuring hug, Unique's cell phone rang. It was Kennard's ring tone.

"Hey, baby," she said, putting the call on speakerphone. She tried to sound cheerful, hoping he wouldn't see through the mask.

"Where are you?" he asked, sounding upbeat.

"Tyeedah's house. School's canceled until further notice," she said.

"Catch a cab to Forty-seventh and Fifth Ave., and I'll drive you back to get the car. The parking down here is ridiculous. I want to show you something, so hurry up and get here. Just call me when you're about to pull up."

"Okay, baby." He obviously wasn't taking no for an answer. "I'm leaving in five minutes."

When she ended the call, Tyeedah was dancing and singing like she had lost her mind. The entire vibe was different.

"What's wrong with you, girl? How you go from shoot 'em bang-bang to Dance Central?"

Unable to contain her exuberance for her friend, she said, "Kennard wants you to meet him at Forty-seventh and Fifth." Unique looked at her like *and?* "That's the Diamond District, girl. As in diamonds, jewels, and stones . . . oh yeah . . . diamonds, jewels, and stones . . ." She sang the words like a nursery rhyme.

"Really?" Unique got a little excited herself.

"Yes, Ms. Thing, *really*."

After giving up on trying to guess what Kennard was up to, Unique asked Tyeedah to help her get a cab. "I'm going to leave my car here," she said.

Tyeedah scooped her house keys up off the counter.

"You know that's a damn shame your country butt still can't hail a cab? Sooner or later we gonna have to get you up to speed on that."

Unique smiled. She would never get used to the yellow-cab lifestyle. Just knowing she was going to a destination without a concrete ride home drove her crazy. That was one of the things she missed about the South. People drove everywhere and there was always free parking.

Once outside, Tyeedah flagged down a taxi in no time. And before Unique pulled off she reminded her one last time, "You have to get that motherfucker before he gets you."

PROMISES AREN'T MADE
TO BE BROKEN

The taxi pulled up at the corner of Forty-seventh Street and Fifth Avenue and Kennard was there to open the door. He helped Unique from the backseat, paid the driver, and kissed her on the cheek.

He asked, "What took you so long?" Before she could mention how congested the traffic was or about the car accident uptown, he said, "Never mind. We have an appointment to keep." He whisked her away by the arm.

Unique had never seen Kennard this excited about anything except making love and money. And not necessarily in that order.

"What's this all about?" His enthusiasm was contagious.

He looked at her with those sexy brown eyes. They were comforting—tender but strong. "I want to buy you something to show the commitment I want to make to you."

Commitment? This is serious, Unique thought as butter-flies took over her stomach at the mention of the word. She had been with many men and none of them had ever mentioned that word.

"Moi?" Her face lit up brighter than the Christmas tree in Rockefeller Center.

"If that means you, then yeah, *moi,"* he said, before kissing her on the forehead. "I was thinking . . ."

"Yes . . . ?" Unique had her own thoughts and they were running butt-naked and wild inside her head. What happened just a few hours ago seemed like a nightmare and she didn't want to think about it. So this gesture could not have come at a better time. She started to question if she even deserved a man like this, but then she thought again, *I've been through more bullshit than Charmin, you gotdamn right I deserve this!*

"I know that we agreed not to talk about either of our past relationships—"

"And we should just focus on *ours,* making it stron-ger," she said, finishing his sentence for him. One she'd heard many times.

But she wasn't expecting what he said next: "I'm glad you broke the agreement last night."

I did what?

"I don't know if you were intoxicated from the champagne or my lovemaking," he joked with a smile.

"I did put it on you, but I'm happy that you opened up. I had no idea that you'd been hurt so badly."

She felt like she'd been hit in the face with a frying pan. Then fear set in. If she didn't have enough to worry about as it was, now she was coughing up skeletons in her sleep. *Damn, I'm really getting way too comfortable.* "Exactly what did I open my mouth up about last night?" she asked, hoping that she didn't look as frightened as she felt.

"You said, and I quote, 'I have never had a *real* relationship and, looking back, I think it fucked up my life.' You also said that you were left to fend for yourself. And that you were double-crossed, in the worst way, by the only man you ever cared for, which made you feel unsure that you would ever be able to trust wholeheartedly again."

Tyeedah was right, Unique thought, *I am falling off.* She was getting as soft as a gay man's dick watching Kim Kardashian's sex tape. She had no idea that she had revealed so much to Kennard last night. He was looking at her now, waiting for her to say something. She was speechless. And maybe keeping her mouth shut was a good thing, only she was a day late and a dollar short.

"That's all true," she managed to say, "but I'm learning to trust. And the more I'm around you it gets easier and easier. . . ."

"Well," Kennard said, beaming, "this is why we're

here. I know we're still in the learning-each-other-phase, not quite ready for an engagement, but I want to make you a promise. A promise to love you and a promise that I will never hurt you, and in addition to that, I want you to know that I will always protect you from your heart . . . and anything that poses a threat to you."

Unique felt like a total fraud for not telling him about this morning. But in her heart she thought it was best, for both of them, especially if she took care of the situation with Fat Tee herself. "I don't know what to say." And that was the truth.

"You don't have to say anything." He led her into a jewelry store. "I'm going to buy you an eye-popping promise ring to remind you of all the promises I've made."

Kennard had a way of making her heart melt and forget about everything in the world except for him.

When the jeweler came over, Kennard said, "Unique, I want you to meet Shummi. Shummi, Unique." Shummi, a Jewish man, was middle-aged, wore a traditional yarmulke and sported Cartier glasses.

"This is interesting, indeed," Shummi said to Kennard with a bright smile. "You told me that you wanted something unique, but you didn't mention that you already had a Unique," he joked. It wasn't funny.

Kennard was ready to get down to business. "Can you show us what you have?"

"Sure! Sure!" Shummi went under the counter into what looked to be a hidden safe and retrieved a case. He sat it atop the counter and opened the lid. The case was filled with stunning rings in various sets and individual diamonds of all shapes and sizes. Against the black cloth the gems sparkled like bright, shiny stars on a dark night. "Now if for some reason you don't like any of these, I'm expecting a few more pieces at any minute and I have an even larger shipment coming on Thursday. All impeccable stones," Shummi proudly said. "I'm talking four carats and up. Real nice stuff. So clear when you look through them, you see clear up to the Niagara Falls."

Unique couldn't imagine that there was something better in quality coming than what he was showing them now. These stones were breathtakingly beautiful. Shummi was explaining each of the diamonds' four Cs—cut, color, carat, and clarity—when someone rang the bell on the door. One of his employees buzzed the person in. It wasn't a customer. The newly arrived person was no more than twenty-one, and had on a bicycle helmet and was wearing a backpack.

Shummi's smile grew even larger than it already was, if that was possible, when he saw the boy enter the store. He handed Unique a beautiful platinum-set ring.

"Total weight nine carats; the center stone is four carats. Very nice stone."

Obviously it had been the one that Kennard had preferred.

"One carat for each of the months we've shared each other's lives," Kennard said. "How do you like it?"

Nine carats! This is one helluva promise, Unique thought. She knew that she and Kennard screwed like rabbits, but who knew he'd treat her like one and supply her with so many damn carats . . . and just the kind she liked? "It's beautiful."

While Unique was admiring the ring, Shummi excused himself for a second. "The courier," he said. "Let me square him away; there may be few other pieces I can show you afterward."

Kennard took a call while Shummi dealt with the courier. Unique continued to look at the ring but couldn't help overhear the conversation between the store owner and delivery boy. She couldn't believe someone would allow diamonds of this quality to be transported by way of bicycle.

But Kennard and Shummi finished up at about the same time. When they all reconvened, a deal was closed. Unique left the store the proud owner of a gorgeous nine-carat promise ring . . . and possibly a way to get some of the money Fat Tee was demanding.

LET THE CARDS FALL
WHERE THEY MAY

Unique's eyes snapped open all of a sudden. She looked over to see that Kennard was still sound asleep. She glanced at the clock on the nightstand. It was four in the morning. It had been a week since Fat Tee had broken into their house and raped, threatened, and tried to extort her, and she had not been able to get a wink of restful sleep whatsoever. Her thoughts were constantly being invaded by how she was going to handle the situation and where she would actually get the money to pay him—or at least enough to get him off her back.

She stole another peek at Kennard, and then she eased out of the bed, trying not to disturb him as she headed for the bathroom. Sitting on the toilet, preparing to pee, she opened the box to take a pregnancy test. She had been a week late and her period had been due to come on the same day Fat Tee had violated her but she hadn't seen a drop of blood anywhere. She was assuming it was the stress she had been going through from the Fat Tee situation. Since he left there a week ago, she had not been able to think of anything else until yesterday when it dawned on her that she had not seen Aunt Flow. The thought of being pregnant was the furthest thing from her mind, but the fact remained that she and Kennard screwed like rabbits, every chance they got, and having unprotected sex most of the time resulted in pregnancy.

Unique peed on the stick, thinking, *Let the cards fall where they may.* So there she sat on the closed toilet lid, waiting for an answer, and almost immediately two pink lines appeared. *Positive! What the fuc—?*

The deck had been stacked against her; the two lines indicated that she was indeed pregnant.

She couldn't move; she just sat there looking spaced-out and dumbfounded, not knowing what she was going to do. It was too soon in her relationship to have a baby, and though she wanted to have kids with Kennard, now wasn't the time. She was only twenty-nine years old, and there were still so many things she wanted to do: finish culinary school, travel the world, and live life to the fullest, and maybe ultimately marry Kennard. Tears trickled down her face. For someone who wasn't a big crier, she seemed to be doing a lot of that lately. How would Kennard feel about all this? She had just started to live this amazing life with him, and she didn't want a baby to be a monkey wrench in it. And most important, she didn't want him to feel like she was trying to trap him with a baby.

Unique was so caught up with deep thoughts that she didn't hear Kennard walk into the bathroom.

"Good morning, gorgeous." He walked over, leaned down, and gave her a kiss; morning breath and all. Out of the corner of his eye, he caught a glimpse of the white stick. "What's this?" he asked, already knowing the answer.

When he picked it up and read the results, his face went completely blank for a second. Unique's fears had come true. She knew it. He wasn't ready for a baby, either. Unique tried to conceal her tears but they disappeared when she saw his expression.

On his face was the biggest, brightest smile she'd ever seen. He gushed, "Baby. This is the best news I've had in a while."

"Really?" Unique said, surprised at his reaction.

"No doubt." He hugged her right there on the toilet. "The greatest news from the greatest girl in the world."

"Awww, baby, I didn't think you wanted kids with all that you have going on. Are you sure the timing of this is right for you?"

Without a moment's hesitation he said, "Couldn't be better." Then his eyes clouded over, dark and heavy. The pall blew away just as suddenly as it surfaced. He motioned for her to get up so he could urinate. She washed her hands while he handled his business and then brushed his teeth. Once he was done he cut off the water, and she gazed deep into his eyes.

"What is it, baby?" She took his hand into hers. "Something's wrong?" He tried to pull it together, but it was too late, she'd seen the brooding in his eyes. He walked into the bedroom and sat on the edge of the bed and once she was positioned beside him, she put her arm around him and gave him a warm look.

"Nine years ago," he said, "I had a girlfriend. Her name was Kyra." Kennard looked at her for a reaction. When he got none, he continued. "I thought I would never be able to love anyone like I loved her, but I was wrong. . . ." His voice was soft. "Because I found you."

"What happened?"

Kennard blew out a jaw full of pent-up air. "I had always dipped and dabbled in the dope game," he said. "When Kyra was seven months pregnant and asked me to give it all up for the sake of the baby, I promised her and myself that I would give up the game the day our baby was born. I'd step into the family business: boxing. My grandfather had been on me to get back in the ring anyway."

"I didn't know you used to box."

Kennard nodded his head. "I'd always been good with my hands, but preferred the business side of the sport more. That's why I became a promoter. Anyway," he said, "Kyra agreed to my terms. And in preparation for my retirement I stepped up my game to another level and got deep in the streets. Got my weight up to an all-time high. Then everything changed. . . ." He bit down on his bottom lip so hard he almost drew blood. This was the first time in the nine-month romance that Unique had ever seen Kennard so vulnerable.

"Babe, are you sure you want to talk about this?"

Again he nodded. "They kidnapped her. They took her and my unborn baby." As if he was looking back into time, he continued, "I know she went kicking and screaming. Kyra was a fighter. . . ." He paused, looked up at Unique, touched her cheek, and said, "Just like you."

Unique listened with a compassionate heart. She rubbed his back to try to ease the pain but clearly it was impossible to do.

"I got a call later that night. Half a million dollars." He looked at her. "That's the value they put on my family."

The question vaulted from her mouth at its own volition. "Did you pay the money?" Unique asked, then regretted it immediately. Was she thinking about Kennard right now or herself?

"I would have given them anything to get my family back," he said. "Even if I had to take the *money* myself. Of course I paid them."

The room became monastery quiet. The next question loomed in the air.

"Then they killed her," he said.

Those words pierced through Unique like an arrow.

"Shot her in the stomach and left her in an abandoned building to bleed out. That shit damn near killed me, too."

Unique couldn't imagine the pain he must've felt when he learned that the woman he loved, and the unborn child he had been anxiously awaiting the arrival of, had been murdered. It was incomprehensible.

A wry smile appeared on his face. "But I kept my word to her: gave up the dope game and got knee-deep in this boxing game, and ended up with all this." He spread out his arms. "Now I have you and another baby on the way. Life really couldn't be better."

Right, she thought as he kissed her on the lips. *Couldn't be better.*

A VICTIM OF CIRCUMSTANCE

Over the next week Kennard doted on Unique. As far as he was concerned, nothing was too good for her—or good enough. Outwardly, Unique basked in his generosity—flowers, candy, notes, jewelry, clothes, food—but inside she felt like a heel for keeping secrets from him. Her conscience ate at her like a tiger dining on slices of raw meat.

But she'd already made up her mind. Now, the shoe was on the other foot, and she had to do what she thought was best for her and her new family.

In Unique's eyes, it was a real blessing in disguise that the big sellout fight was less than two weeks away. The upcoming festivities kept Kennard extremely busy. This was being called the fight of the decade and Kennard was milking it for all that it was worth. Set to take place in Madison Square Garden, the sheer magnitude of the event kept him away from Unique more than usual.

The timing couldn't have been better. Unique

hated not seeing him until late at night, but the time alone was perfect for putting her own business in order. After playing and replaying the pros and cons in her mind over and over, she decided that the only logical option was to heist Shummi's diamonds. She liked Shummi a lot and the man had never done anything to her, but what else could she do? Her back was up against the wall. It was the only way to get Fat Tee off of her back and out of her life.

And with that being said, today was the day it was about to go down, and she had solicited Tyeedah and her little brother for help.

All I can say is love makes a person do some strange shit!

Unique waited on Fifty-second Street for the courier to pass. She had his schedule down pat like the finale to a tango. Once she saw him bend the corner, Unique knew there was no turning back. It was about to go down. She felt bad that she had to do this but was relieved that this was going to finally be over once and for all.

Once Unique saw the courier, she spoke into her Bluetooth. "There he goes: blue jeans, camouflage jacket, and a Jets baseball cap. Game on, Playboy."

"Roger that," Lil-Bro said from a motorized scooter. He confirmed he had seen the target. "I got him."

Unique quickly hopped into a pedicab and instructed the guy to take her to Fifth Avenue. The man maneuvered the three-wheeled passenger bicycle with great precision while she still had the courier in sight. He started weaving in and out of the afternoon traffic, seemingly unfazed by the congestion and poisonous exhaust fumes and diesel fuel he breathed in from the clusters of cabs and buses polluting the atmosphere. Lil-Bro was in and out of traffic as well, trailing the courier on his moped. Traffic came to a halt but it didn't stop him. The courier, used to sharing the crowded streets with many modes of transportation, didn't think anything of the moped on his tail.

In between buses and alongside cabs, Lil-Bro rode that motorbike like he was in a triathlon, trailing the courier like he was racing for the medal.

In the process of coming to the surprise stop, Lil-Bro ran up beside the messenger and bumped the back wheel of his bike by mistake, causing him to lose control of the bike and fly over the handlebars and hit the concrete.

"Oh shit!" Lil-Bro said, quickly stopping his own moped. "Man, I'm sorry!" He added, as innocently as possible. "I was texting and riding, man . . . you know how that shit is." Lil-Bro got off his bike and began to help the man off the ground. "I feel bad, man. Hope I ain't bruise your ego."

The jewel mule, upset from the fall and even more distracted by Lil-Bro's grungy-looking appearance, never felt the needle prick the skin on the back of his neck as he was being helped up. Lil-Bro was so swift that he should have been a nurse or a doctor the way he pulled it off. Unique watched and even she missed the sight of the syringe. She had to admit Lil-Bro was smooth.

Instinctively, the courier felt for the satchel that was still safely around his neck. "Yeah, I'm good," he said, getting back on the bike, trying to get his focus back on his route.

Lil-Bro's role was vital—when he took that syringe filled with the date-rape drug and injected it straight into the courier's bloodstream, everything was going as planned. "On the road again," he said into his Blue-tooth to tell his sister and Unique. "Coming your way now, Big Sis." He let the girls know that it was all about to unfold.

After two more blocks, the double dose of the date-rape drug began to take effect quicker than they thought. Judging by the way the courier was riding he had a low-tolerance for narcotics. He swerved and then almost fell off the bike, which let the trio know that the courier was well ahead of schedule. The mes-senger seemed to be discombobulated and it was clear that he was going to go down soon. Unique was close by, trailing behind him in her bicycle-drawn carriage. It was time for her to be rid of her chariot and be on foot. She alerted the driver, "Pull over here up ahead."

She paid him and got off. "Game on, girly!" she said to Tyeedah.

Another block away, Tyeedah was also on foot, waiting for the messenger to bend the corner and when he did, people were lined on both sides of the streets in the middle of rush hour.

As soon as the courier hit the ground, Lil-Bro darted in front of a Nissan and caused an accident himself, running smack-dead into a yellow cab and making himself fall to the ground and appear injured. Some people saw him and stopped to look, but most people minded their own business and went about their merry way. Unique looked over her shoulder and couldn't believe how nobody really was paying attention. "You gotta love this city," she murmured aloud.

"Girls, you're on your own," he said into the Bluetooth, but he kept it moving, not looking back. He'd done his part.

By now, the courier was on the ground, clueless as to what was going on or what happened to him. As soon as he fell to the hard concrete, Unique and Tyeedah went into action.

"Oh my God, somebody call an ambulance!" Unique exclaimed, right after Tyeedah had grabbed the courier's bag from around his neck and headed to hail down a cab. He was too out of it to even try to put up a fight. In fact, he was sweating and about to pass out.

The minute somebody else stopped, she left the bystanders there to deal with the poor diamondless guy.

She couldn't believe it was as easy as taking candy from a baby, or in this case, taking carats from a rabbit. Unique smiled; she couldn't believe how simple it was. She mixed into the crowd and hopped in the cab, and she and Tyeedah fled the scene like bandits.

LET'S GET DOWN TO BUSINESS

An hour later the girls were in a booth, waiting on Fat Tee. Tyeedah had refused to allow Unique to go alone to deal with the jackass. The coffee shop was crowded with patrons trying to boost their already high and unhealthy caffeine levels.

"That's him." Unique nodded to Tyeedah. Fat Tee walked in, wearing a wrinkled Willie Esco jean outfit that looked like he had slept in it. The girls didn't even have the common courtesy to motion to him; they let him look lost as he searched the coffee shop for Unique. Once he laid his eyes on them, he grinned that aluminum smile as soon as he saw Unique. Then he headed over to where they were sitting.

"Damn, girl, that's what I always loved about you, Unique," he said, plopping down in the booth seat on Tyeedah's side, opposite of Unique. He was excited. "Anything you put your head to, you make happen. You are one of the most ambitious people I know, I will say that," he said, feeling the vibe that Unique had really pulled off getting him his million dollars. "You know I give props where they are due."

Unique just sat there with no emotion toward Fat Tee as he tried to act like a big shot.

"Who's your friend?" He looked Tyeedah up and down and licked his lips. "Fine ass. You know the freaky things I'd do to you, girl?"

Tyeedah glared at him, and her nose flared like someone had just dropped a bag of shit next to her. "Not in your wildest dream or nightmare for that matter," she responded, shutting him down.

Unique never offered a name; Fat Tee already knew too much for his own good. Fat Tee kept eyeballing Tyeedah, obviously feeling himself, but Unique wasn't bothered by that. "How about you let me take you down south with my friend," he said with an exaggerated drawl, painting his crusty, purple lips with his tongue.

Tyeedah snorted. "If you were dying of starvation, I wouldn't even allow you to eat out of my ass."

Not sure whether he should take the remark as a compliment or a diss, Fat Tee was at a loss for words. His mouth parted but no words came out; the look on his face was priceless.

"Let's get down to business, don't nobody have time to be shucking and jiving with you. This is not a leisure session, this is a business meeting," Unique said, and handed him a Bergdorf Goodman shopping bag, which contained the knapsack with the diamonds in it.

Fat Tee looked confused and asked, "What the fuck is this? Ain't no million fucking dollars in here."

"Actually, it's more than a million dollars," Unique said dryly. She looked around to make sure no one had heard his loud voice before she spoke again. "Just open it up and look in the bag."

When he did, the sheen from the diamonds seemed to lighten up the entire room. His eyes did a double take. "What the fuck is this?"

"This fool can't be as stupid as he was acting," Tyeedah said to Unique.

"What does it look like?" Unique asked Fat Tee mockingly.

"I know what they are," Fat Tee acknowledged, "but what the fuck I'm supposed to do with them? I asked for cash."

There were over a hundred diamonds in the pouch, all either nicer or just as nice as the ones that Shummi showed to her and Kennard. Unique's mental appraisal of the jewels was that they were worth way over a million dollars. *Damn, I'm so wanting to get this nigga off my back that I'm slipping.* In fact, Unique was disappointed in herself that she wished in hindsight that she had taken out a few of the diamonds for herself; at least she could have given Tyeedah and Lil-Bro a couple for their help. But she just wanted to get Fat Tee out of her face, out of her life, and on his way.

"What the fuck you think you're supposed to do with them? They are fucking some of the best diamonds available," she informed him. "You still a hustler, right?" she said sarcastically.

He looked at her like she was asking him the most stupid question. "Until the day I die. But that don't have shit to do with the fact that I asked for cash. Hell, you might as well have given me fuckin' euros that I have to go to the foreign currency counter to exchange. I wanted cash."

Tyeedah sucked her teeth and added, "Again, are you sure you a hustla? Or a pimp? 'Cause it's a little confusing to me."

That comment bothered Fat Tee, and he used his neck to motion to Unique. "She knows my résumé in the streets?"

"Résumé? I can't tell? You asking her what you gonna do with some diamonds. Who knows? Shit, you stalking ladies for money and shit—ain't no real hustla raping and extorting no woman for money," Tyeedah said, wanting to give him more than a piece of her mind.

Unique spoke up before this got out of control. "Just like coke, dope, weed, guns, or whatever you moving these days, you hustle these but the return on these beauties is going to be so much more than anything you ever grinded in your life."

"It didn't cost you nothing, so the only thing you gotta recoup is that Chinese bus ticket you got to get yo ass up here and that roach motel you staying at," Tyeedah said, dead serious.

Fat Tee brushed the last comment off and was thinking about what Unique said. Then it dawned on her that the fool had never seen this many precious stones in his life, outside of a movie. But that wasn't her problem and she continued to sell the gems to him. "They're top-notch cuts and the clarity is ridiculous. Well over millions of dollars retail." She looked in his eyes. "Do it right . . . ," she assured him with sincerity, "and you'll come off with a million plus."

Unique could tell by Fat Tee's blank expression that he had no idea if what she was saying was true or if she was just shooting game to him. Fat Tee sold drugs and dealt in cash; that's all he really knew. "Look, I'm not blowing smoke up your ass. I wish we could keep them for myself. I'm just trying to make this right because what Took did was wrong," she said genuinely.

"She putting you onto something new and at this point; what do you have to lose?" Tyeedah asked.

Unique's patience was growing thin with all this back-and-forth with Fat Tee, and she was about to tell him to take it or leave it when her cell phone went off.

It was Kennard calling. This wasn't the time or place to take his call. But it *was* her cue to end this meeting and get the hell out of there. For good. "I think our business is done," she said. "I have a life to go live now that this chapter is closed." She got up to leave.

Fat Tee stayed seated. "I think I'll stay for a cup of espresso."

He was blocking Tyeedah in. "Excuse me," she said.

He played dumb. "My bad." Or maybe he wasn't playing. He stood up so that Tyeedah could pass. When she did, Fat Tee smacked her on her behind.

Tyeedah shot him a look like she wanted to cut his head off with a dull knife right there in the coffee shop. "That's your first and last time ever touching me," she said, with the words of dynamite.

Fat Tee rolled his eyes and Unique stepped in. "Let's go, girl." Unique pulled Tyeedah by the arm. "He's not worth the drama. Like I said, our business here with this Bozo is done." Unique walked out of the coffee shop with Tyeedah, satisfied that she'd righted a wrong and had gotten a bitch-ass nigga off of her back in the process.

It was too bad that Fat Tee had other plans.

THE HOOPLA

It was Thursday, two days before the big fight. It had been a couple of weeks since the big news that she and Kennard were expecting their first child and Unique seemed to be glowing. She wasn't showing any signs of a baby bump but with Fat Tee off her back, she was starting to embrace the fact that she was indeed about to bring a life into the world. And she was the first to admit that it was a scary thought.

It was standing room only at the grand ballroom of the Tabby Hotel. Unique sat in her seat, positioned between Tyeedah and Kennard's mother, Katie, who loved Unique and thought that she was a lovely Southern belle. In Ms. Katie's eyes, the girl was a godsend to her son and could do nothing wrong. The conservative lady would go into a cardiac arrest if she knew that Unique was no angel and had been to hell and back.

They were there for the press conference in preparation for the big fight at Madison Square Garden. With a sellout crowd and all the hoopla and hype surrounding the fight, Unique wondered what more press could they really need?

Both boxers had outsized personalities and backstories that lent themselves to characters created for television, and this event was staged for pure entertainment. Rumor had it that both fighters had been offered reality shows on VH1.

The champ was Jockney Jang, who was signed to Kennard's management company although on paper he belonged to Ms. Katie. The Muhammad Ali Boxing Reform Act didn't permit promoters to manage and promote boxers, so this was the way to maneuver around that rule. Jang had been with Knockout Management for eight years. He had an undefeated record and was known for his flamboyance and trash talk.

He punished the guys who got in the ring with him and afterward would feel so bad about the damage that he'd done that he'd often send flowers and letters of apology to some of his opponents' mothers and wives for having to witness their loved ones take such an embarrassing beat down in front of them.

His opponent was a guy who, three years ago, no one thought would ever fight another match that didn't involve him in taking a dive. At that time, Taymar Woodley was nothing more than just another washed-up boxer who appeared to lose his drive and passion for the art of boxing. The rumor mill had it that his sole purpose for even being in the ring was to get the IRS off his back and get current with child-support payments to all his babies' mothers.

One day, Kennard and Taymar were talking about life and the sport in general.

Taymar said he wished he had a chance to do it all over again, how he would train like there was no end and never take anything for granted. Would've, should've, and could've were all Taymar kept saying, as Kennard listened attentively to him.

For years, Kennard had seen something in this man that Taymar didn't even see in himself anymore: a champion.

Kennard decided that since odds had always been in his favor, he'd take his chances and roll the dice on Taymar. The guy just needed the right people in his corner, and it started with the trainer.

Kennard's dad, Bernard, was the best of the best when it came to training champions. Bernard had been in the boxing game since he was ten years old. He started out as a prizefighter and went on to become one of the best trainers in the sport. Then one day, he gave up training professional boxers to dedicate all of his time and money to giving back to the youth, training underprivileged kids to become Olympic-quality fighters and even better men became his new passion.

Bernard had high expectations and big dreams for his only son, Kennard, who was once a boxing phenom himself. He'd never lost a fight all the way through the Junior Olympics, generating huge buzz. Everybody in boxing knew that Bernard's boy was destined for stardom and would one day become the heavyweight champion. There was no doubt that Kennard had the potential to exceed any of his father's expectations, if only it was what *he* wanted.

The problem was, at the time, Kennard was sixteen and being a champion in the ring *wasn't* what he wanted. That was his father's dream and his father's father's. Not at all his.

Kennard's dream at the time was to be a street champion. He was more interested in running the block than moving around in the ring. Eventually he lost his focus for boxing, and instead redirected his attention to building a drug empire.

But after his girl and unborn child were kidnapped and murdered, Kennard got back into boxing, fulfilling his promise to Kyra. To channel his frustrations, he went to the boxing gym faithfully, but this time around, he took interest in the business end. At first, Bernard was still upset that his son, a natural boxer, had thrown away his career, but he couldn't deny that the boy's business sense was impeccable.

He had all the qualities a good businessman

needed: he was funny, charming, calculating, smart on many levels, egotistical, demanding, and slightly neurotic. All these components made him a force to be reckoned with. He could cause a vertigo effect on people by talking circles around them if they weren't careful. For this reason alone, most people preferred to negotiate with Kennard on paper or across the e-mail.

Kennard had to convince his father to come out of retirement and train Taymar, but it wasn't easy.

"Dude is washed up," Bernard had said, when his son first brought up the idea.

Kennard looked at his father dead-on. "Well, if anyone can bring him back, you can, Pop. You won't be sorry."

"Do you know the difference between a dream and a fairy tale, son?" he said. "Dreams are meant to be achieved. Fairy tales are to be believed."

"I see it slightly different, Dad. I think that dreams are meant to be believed, as well. However, fairy tales are meant to convince someone else to believe *in* them."

Bernard chuckled. "I think we're saying the same thing."

"I feel strongly about this, Pop. But, make no mistake about it; I'm going to need your help to pull it off."

Bernard said that he would think about it and then walked away. Kennard was sure that Pops would do it, but knew better than to press his father. The man was as stubborn as he was a good trainer. A week later, Bernard sat Kennard down.

"You really believe in this guy?" The question had come from left field as far as Kennard was concerned. He thought his father had dismissed the idea altogether.

"Yeah, Pop. I do." Kennard could barely contain his smile. "Call it a hunch."

Kennard and his father didn't always see eye to eye, but Bernard loved his son more than life itself, and he believed in his son's instincts.

Bernard signed on as Taymar's trainer; Kennard signed the fighter to Knockout Management. Taymar understood that this was his last chance. With the father-son duo behind him, if he listened to them, his financial woes would be a thing of the past. And since that time Taymar didn't look back, only down on the chumps unlucky enough to get in the ring with him.

Unique had to admit, she was enjoying the festivities. Not only were both boxers signed to Kennard's management company, he was one of the promoters as well. Her man was a genius when it came to making money. And he was a stallion in bed.

When Taymar walked on the stage, he was carrying a big, beautifully wrapped gold box with a black bow, which he handed to Jang. "I bought you a present," he said into the microphone, for everyone to hear.

Jang played along, good sport and all.

"You shouldn't have," he said.

Jang opened the box. A sheepish smirk appeared on his face once he looked inside. A wreath of flowers, the kind mourners send to funerals. Taymar had beaten him at his own game.

The card read: FOR THE COUNT OF TEN. REST IN PEACE!

Unique was enjoying herself, sitting beside her future mother-in-law . . . all the way up until she looked over her shoulder. Fat Tee was there, with a Kool-Aid grin plastered on his face. *What the fuck did he want now?* All Unique knew was she wasn't going to dare let him come over and approach her, with Ms. Katie sitting there to witness whatever recklessness he had to say.

Ms. Katie could see the look on Unique's face. "You look like you've seen a ghost. Are you okay, dear?"

"What's wrong?" Tyeedah asked, sensing something wasn't right.

"I have to go to the restroom. I think I'm going to be sick." Unique stormed off quickly. She knew she had to leave the press conference because she didn't want any confusion between her and Fat Tee to pop off especially since Kennard was within a fifty-foot radius.

Ms. Katie was about to direct Tyeedah to go with Unique, but Tyeedah could already sense that something was wrong and was hot on Unique's heels. Fat Tee followed them both.

Outside of the ballroom in the lobby of the hotel, there were a few people hanging out but they were caught up in the festivities and didn't pay them any mind. Fat Tee stopped them in their tracks right outside the ladies' restroom.

He called out, "Ayo, I need to talk to you."

Unique spun around. "We have nothing to talk about. I told you two weeks ago, our business is over," she said discreetly, not wanting to draw any unnecessary attention to them. Tyeedah just crossed her arms over her chest, watching with contempt.

"It's over when I say it's over." He leaned in and said to Unique in a low tone, "And the fat lady hasn't even warmed up her pipes yet."

"What do you want now?" Unique asked. At that second, she regretted refusing to take Tyeedah's advice from the beginning.

"Besides an early death," Tyeedah mumbled under her breath.

Fat Tee shot a look at Tyeedah to blow her off, then focused back on Unique, and leaned in even closer, and firmly told her, "You gone set that nigga up for me, just like you did me for Took. Same shit, just different day, different people."

"Are you crazy? Fuck outta here, I'm not doing that shit," she blurted out, not caring if people heard her. She thought that she was going to be sick but it took everything in her to not go crazy and make a scene.

"Don't play dumb, bitch." He was so angry that when he spoke, a slight bit of slobber came out of his mouth and went onto her blouse.

Unique glared straight into his eyes and spoke slowly. She wanted to be sure he comprehended. "Listen to me. It's. Not. Fucking. Happening. You heard me? I repeat: Not. Fucking. Happening."

He stepped toward her as if he was about to hit her, but she was quicker than him. She was prepared and showed him the business end of the pistol that she had tucked in her purse. "If you come near me again, I promise you on everything I love and hate, that I will kill your bitch ass." She had tried to make it right, but all she got for her troubles were more troubles. No more. She was tired of being the nice bitch.

He searched her eyes, looking for a sign that she was bluffing. The anger and rage written all over her face combined with fire in her eyes, let him know that this wasn't a poker game, and bluffing . . . she wasn't.

One of the many extra security guards hired for

the event noticed the commotion. He walked over and made his presence known. He was huge, six foot six and built like a truck. He asked, "Y'all good?" directing the question to the ladies. He was gritting on Fat Tee like he was itching for some reaction. Those two measly words spoke volumes.

Unique kept her eyes on Fat Tee, but said, "Yeah, we good."

FADED TO BLACK

Since the Tabby was hosting a lot of the major events associated with the fight of the decade, Kennard booked in advance more than a hundred rooms for the week for his VIP friends and guests, including the Presidential Suite for himself and Unique.

While Kennard was running around doing a million things, Unique was relaxing under the masseuse-like pellets of hot water spraying from the hotel's custom showerheads. She vacillated over whether or not she should come clean with Kennard about being accosted by Fat Tee yesterday. If she did, then she would have to tell Kennard about everything. But did she really want to open that can of worms? And hell, from the beginning God made it clear that man didn't need to know everything. *So why should I play devil's advocate and give Kennard a bite of the apple? Some things were just better left unknown.*

Fortunately for Unique, last-minute details had Kennard ripping and running so they had next to no time alone all week. The night before when he finally came to bed, all he wanted to do was make love, but he was so tired he could barely do that.

Still, Unique knew that she would have to open up to Kennard and tell him sooner rather than later. The last thing she wanted was for someone else that may have witnessed the incident in the lobby to tell him first . . . or worse, for Fat Tee to manage to bump into him and drop a dime of the details of her checkered past plus God knows what else. How would that look? Like she was keeping secrets, that's how—which she was. The problem with secrets, she thought, was that they ate at one's conscience bit by bit. If one wasn't careful they could consume one's entire life. One secret oftentimes led to another, then another, multiplying like rabbits.

Unique couldn't take it: her mind was made up, she couldn't hold water anymore. She made a promise to herself as she rinsed off the luxurious shower gel that she was going to tell Kennard everything. Every single sordid detail of her past—well, at least the Fat Tee and Took episodes. So just as Eve had done with Adam, she would practically hand-feed him the forbidden fruit. Let the core fall where it may, because she would leave no seed unplanted. She'd tell him it all . . . well, maybe not *every* shiesty detail.

She'd talk about the robberies she and Took pulled

off together. She would even share how while they were supposedly on a romantic vacation, Took had drugged her and then sold her to a whorehouse in Mexico for a key of cocaine and a chicken, leaving her with no passport but wanted by the law in the United States. He didn't do it because he needed the drugs, and he sure as hell wasn't hungry. He did it because he had a warped sense of humor and no sense of forgiveness. The funny thing, Unique thought, as her mind conjured up vivid memories of the past like a blooper reel of her life, was that although she was pissed to the highest level of pissitivity for what Took had done, she knew, deep down, that she deserved his treachery. She had crossed that invisible but very tangible line of trust first. She, too, had convinced herself that his actions were only a reaction to her action.

If Kennard wasn't run off by then, she would also finally come clean about Fat Tee. How she and Took robbed him back in the day. How Fat Tee found her by seeing her on ESPN. Leaving the note on her Benz, following her, breaking into their house, raping and then blackmailing her. The stolen diamonds to get Fat Tee off her back, which obviously didn't work.

She would leave no stone unturned. No more secrets. If Kennard left her, which he probably would if he had any sense, so be it. At least she would be at peace with herself. And if he stayed, which was a long shot, but if he did, their relationship would be stronger for it. They could truly be a family—him, her, and the baby growing inside her stomach.

Knowing that there was no perfect time to confess something as complex and of this magnitude, she decided to do it after the fight tomorrow night. No need to destroy the man's mood before one the biggest milestones in his professional career.

One more day to pretend, but right now all she could do was get herself together, put her game face on, and focus on the here and now. Turning the volume on the shower radio up—tuned to Hot 97—she closed her eyes and let the water cascade over her face and the rest of her body.

The built-in steamer inside the shower melted away some of the stress she felt. The weigh-in for the fight was this evening, and Unique had agreed to meet Kennard downstairs at 6 P.M. for photos. In another hour her makeup team would arrive, and thirty minutes later, Tyeedah would be knocking on the door.

Unique had chosen a stunning custom-made dress for tonight, a prelude to the eye-popping, body-hugging peek-a-boo she planned to debut tomorrow. She rubbed the soapy sponge across her flat stomach, which was hard and toned. She worked diligently in the gym to keep her body in tip-top shape. The fight would probably be her last stage to flaunt it before she started showing a baby bump.

She planned to make the most of it.

Entertainment Tonight, Extra, and *Inside Edition* had already asked Kennard for interviews, and Unique wanted to look her best in case they flashed the camera on her. Unless there was a crime against being drop-dead fabulous, she had no worries about being criticized by any of the glorified tabloids' in-house fashion police.

Just as Unique was finishing her shower, the lights went out, blanketing the bathroom into complete darkness. She figured Kennard had come back up and caught her in the shower and was in a joking mood.

"Ha-ha, Kennard, real funny. Now turn the lights back on. I'm running late as it is," she said, while trying to feel for the knob to turn the water off.

"Maybe you will think this is funny now." The voice shocked the hell out of her. It wasn't Kennard.

Fear replaced the water enveloping her entire body and within a blink of an eye, a pair of hands ripped her from the shower and then punched her in the face so hard it rattled her teeth.

"Where's your pistol now, bitch?"

Unique absorbed the punch and was still on her feet. Hell, if she made it through this mess, maybe she'd be Kennard's next big prizefighter. She could take a blow, that was for sure. And to take a blow of that magnitude from a dude like a champ showed that if she was in the ring with a broad she'd definitely make it to the final round. But then again, hadn't she always been the last bitch standing?

"You ain't bad now, is ya, bitch?"

She wondered how in the hell Fat Tee had gotten into her secured hotel room. And why had she left the gun in her purse in the chair? Of course, she hadn't expected a maniac to break into the room of a five-star hotel's Presidential Suite.

The initial shock of the moment waning, Unique took a looping right-handed swing that clipped Fat Tee on the chin. To spend extra quality time with Kennard and to stay in shape, she had taken boxing and self-defense classes at the boxing gym. The trainer had said she was a natural. But with the slippery floor under bare, wet feet, she wasn't stable enough to create the force behind the blow that she tried to throw.

Fat Tee wasted no time landing another sledge-hammer against her temple. This time, Unique's legs wobbled like a bowl of cheap ramen noodles before quitting on the job.

Once Unique hit the cold marble floor, Fat Tee dropped down on top of her, knees straddling her upper body. The bastard moved around like he had been slithering in the dark all of his life. Who knew shit would play out like this? But then again, Unique should have known, for it had already been written.

"I told you this wasn't over until I said it was over. But you wanted to play rough. So," he said, with one hand around her neck and the other holding her wrists above her head, "I'll show you what the fuck rough looks like, bitch."

She could smell the Hennessy on his breath.

Unique wanted to beat herself up for underestimating Fat Tee, but there was no time for woulda-shouldas. Besides, Fat Tee had literally beaten her to the punch anyway.

But regardless of how daunting the situation seemed, she didn't intend to be raped by Fat Tee again. Unique was going to fight with everything she had—for herself and for the baby growing inside of her.

Fat Tee had enough pressure on her neck to prevent her from screaming. And she could barely breathe. The hold was similar to the way he had handled her when he had overtaken her at the house. But this time Unique was determined not to let him achieve the same results. One was her maximum limit in this lifetime to be raped by this stupid fuck-off.

"It didn't have to be this way," he said.

Unique tried to speak but the words couldn't get past the grip he had on her neck.

Fat Tee sensed that she was trying to say something, and he loosened his grip . . . slightly. Unique mumbled, but there was no way he could discern what she was saying. She couldn't even recognize the garbled words as they squeezed through her windpipe.

"What did you say, bitch?"

She heard the greed in his voice. He probably thought she was giving in, trying to tell him how he could rob Kennard.

She spewed off a few more, low words.

Fat Tee bent over, placing his ear closer to her mouth so that he could hear better. He wasn't taking any chances by loosening the choke hold, allowing her to scream for help.

The side of his head was inches from Unique's face.

She raised her head to get closer. Close enough to kiss him if she wanted to. Instead, Unique clamped onto the lobe of Fat Tee's ear with her teeth. He screamed, "Ouch, bitch," but she held on like a mother pit bull fighting for her pups. Yanking her head, she tore a chunk of his ear away, kindred to the way Mike Tyson disfigured Evander Holyfield in the ring.

Fat Tee screeched like a wounded mutt and jerked back, which gave her just enough to—with all the strength in her body—swing her knee upward, Tae-Bo style, toward his petite dick. Praying that size didn't matter, she felt the softness of his testicles crunch under the hard bone of her kneecap.

Fat Tee sang in soprano, curling up on his side.

Unique hurried to her feet before Fat Tee recovered and headed toward a sliver of light, peeking under the bathroom door. She took off toward the light. Her mind quickly ran through her options. She had no time to get dressed, and Fat Tee would be back on his feet at any minute. She either had to flee the hotel room naked and get help, or retrieve the gun from her purse and help herself.

She was no more than two feet from the light—near freedom—when Fat Tee grabbed her ankle. She tried to stomp his hand with her free foot, but she hit a slippery spot on the floor and her feet skated from beneath her. She lost her balance.

Regaining his composure, Fat Tee was back on top of her. He slammed his fist into her face so hard she thought she saw the Big Dipper. She raked at his face with her nails. She felt the manicured claws dig into his flesh. She smelled his blood, or maybe it was her own blood—no, she was sure it was his—but Fat Tee kept pounding her with blow after blow until Unique eventually faded to black. When Fat Tee finally stopped, he realized that she wasn't moving and all he saw was a puddle of blood. He smiled because he never thought in a million years that Unique would ever go out like a blood bitch. He washed his hands and looked at Unique's lifeless body bleeding out on the floor, and said, "What goes around comes around, bitch."

UNIQUE II: BETRAYAL

PROLOGUE

The queen-sized bed took up more than half of the space in the rented seedy hotel room. The other half contained a night table, matching dresser with a mirror, a miniature coffee table, and an armoire that housed a flat-screen TV behind its French-style doors. In the corner was a small dorm-room-sized refrigerator. Fat Tee sat at the old, rickety coffee table, which had seen better days, drinking a Heineken that the fridge had barely kept cold. Fat Tee had thought about getting a room at one of the upscale hotels now that he had a few dollars, but the plus side to staying at Bugley's Inn was that it was inexpensive by New York standards, and for the most part the people that squatted there were too busy minding their own business to mind his.

God knows he had enough problems as it was and the last thing he needed was someone up in his business. When Fat Tee had first driven his late model Honda to New York in search of Unique, all he wanted was a little revenge for what she and her ex-boyfriend Took had done to him over seven years ago. After three months of searching the big city's seedy areas and not locating her, Fat Tee had been ready to call it a waste of time. Then, sitting in this very same room, he saw an ESPN special on Kennard DuVall. The strikingly beautiful woman by Kennard's side caught his eye as the cameras followed them through their New Jersey mansion. Fat Tee had to do a double and then a triple take. Fat Tee kept telling himself, "Naw, it couldn't be." He sat in total silence and studied the woman. It wasn't until Kennard looked at the woman with a smile of a nigga who had been pussy-whipped and said, "Unique is the love of my life," that Fat Tee knew for sure.

Immediately Fat Tee knew that there was only one bitch by that name capable of casting that type of spell over such a powerful man. Unique was as beautiful as she was conniving, maybe more.

This changed things for Fat Tee tremendously. Back in Virginia seven years ago, after Took and Unique had scammed him, a trail of bad luck seemed to follow him. Once one of the most hood-richest dudes to walk the streets of Richmond, Virginia, he was now down and out with a dope habit and a docket full of court cases, with no money to pay for the drugs or a lawyer. He had ended up going to prison and kicking his habit.

While some used jail time to rehabilitate themselves, Fat Tee couldn't focus on bettering himself. All he could seem to think about was getting out of jail and getting even with Unique for not only hurting his feelings but bruising his ego and stealing his livelihood.

When he found out the fact that Unique was dating Kennard DuVall, the stakes were quickly raised.

It wasn't hard to find Unique after the ESPN piece aired. The very next day, Fat Tee just waited outside of Kennard's office building until, lo and behold, Unique rolled up, driving a shiny red Benz. He followed her to the house she and Kennard shared in Jersey. His daddy used to install alarms so bypassing the security system was a breeze for Fat Tee. He probably should have followed in his father's footsteps or at least chosen a different career path, he thought, but hindsight was always twenty-twenty.

The look on Unique's face when she saw him in their house was priceless. That little housecoat she had on barely covered her perfectly round behind. He couldn't resist, and for old times' sake, Fat Tee roughed off and straight sexually violated her at gunpoint. And before he left he had demanded a million dollars not to expose her secrets to her rich fiancé.

So happy with her new life with Kennard, Unique had been willing to do anything not to disclose her past to him. It was no surprise when Unique—with the help of Tyeedah—dug into her old bag of tricks and came up with a plan to intercept a bag of high-quality diamonds from a courier before the diamonds were delivered to their intended destination, which was Kennard's very own jeweler. Unique gave every last one of the diamonds to Fat Tee to get him off her back in hopes that he would carry his washed-up ass back down I-95 to Virginia.

Dumping the stolen diamonds proved to be a super-sized headache for Fat Tee. What was the worth of one hundred and forty-five flawless diamonds, all three carats or better?

Retail value: almost two million, but on an open market with no buyers: zero.

If Fat Tee didn't want a first-class ticket on a Grey Goose straight to somebody's prison yard, he knew that he had to be patient and move the diamonds slow. One at a time if that's what it took. Three weeks went by before he'd made his first successful transaction. So far, he had sold four—two each to a couple of shady diamond dealers downtown—which meant that there were still a hundred and forty-one to go. The weight of the $20K in his pocket gave him the inspiration to stay the course. He flipped his initial idea of hightailing it back to the R to get rid of the stones there, but dismissed the notion after deeper thought. Sure, he would feel more comfortable and would be able to maneuver more in Richmond, but comfort damn sure didn't mean an easier task.

The loud rapping, knuckles banging against the room's door, startled him. The fact that the knock wasn't followed by, "Open up! Police!" and that the door was still on its hinges was a good sign. He didn't believe in that type of stuff—hunches, signs, and all that—but he should've.

Fat Tee rose, broke off the four steps it took to get from where he was seated to the door. "Who is it?" he said.

The voice from the other side answered back, "Bone."

This was the dude Fat Tee had been waiting on.

Still talking through the door. "You by yourself?"

"Didn't think it was that type of party. But I can go get a few more people, if you want," Bone said. "Ain't no big deal, partna."

Fat Tee slid the dead bolt to the left, then released the lock. "Just being cautious," he said once he'd opened the door. "Come on in."

The guy crossing the threshold was six foot two, brown-skinned, with a close haircut. Bone looked to be in his early thirties, around the same age as Fat Tee. He carried a small zip-up bag in his right hand. Noticing that Fat Tee's eyes were glued to it, Bone said, "The money," as he walked by.

Fat Tee nodded. "Like I said—" he closed the door and slid the dead bolt back home "—just being cautious."

The room grew quiet with distrust and suspicion, even though the two of them had been introduced by a mutual friend of a friend. It was simple: Fat Tee had diamonds he was trying to sell and Bone had money that he was trying to spend on diamonds. The time and place was arranged over the phone, but this was the first time the two men were meeting face-to-face.

Bone broke the awkward silence. "Mind if I see what I came to buy?" He sat in the same seat, at the worn coffee table, that Fat Tee had been keeping warm earlier. He tried to act casual, but he had busy eyes.

Digging in the front right pocket of his jeans, Fat Tee pulled out a small black felt pouch and tossed it to Bone. Bone's eyes tracked the pass like a sure-handed receiver and he made the catch easily.

With his index fingers, Bone wedged the top open and then poured the contents of the pouch into his palm. The brilliance from the diamonds in Bone's hand twinkled like a new sunrise. He was impressed. He took one of the diamonds from his palm and with his thumb and index finger, rolled the stone back and forth like he was priming his woman's erect nipple. He licked his lips lustfully as he marveled at its beauty.

With his eyes still on the prize, Bone said, "How many more of these babies do you have on you?"

Fat Tee wasn't that stupid by a long shot; he'd only brought three diamonds for this meeting's first show-and-tell. The other hundred and forty-one stones were upstairs on another floor, in a second room he rented.

"Only the three," Fat Tee lied. "But I can make a call. Get a few more sent up from Richmond"—he looked into Bone's eyes—"if the price is right," reminding Bone that he had yet to see any money to complete the transaction at hand.

Responding to the not-so-subtle hint in a tone that sounded as if he was offended, Bone said, "My cheddar's good, bee. Ask around." To prove the point, Bone reached for the bag he'd brought into the room, the one he said contained the money and unzipped it. Knowing good and well that a pistol could have found a home inside just as easily as the money, Fat Tee was on edge, his muscles tightening. He didn't relax until Bone dumped what looked like four ten-thousand-dollar stacks out on the table. More than enough to pay for the three diamonds he held in his palm. "And there's plenty more where this comes from," Bone said.

Jackpot, Fat Tee thought to himself.

They'd already negotiated, in the blind, on seven thousand dollars a pop for the diamonds per satisfaction on sight. Judging by the smile on Bone's face, apparently he was satisfied and ready to do more business.

Rather than let the other nineteen grand walk back out the door, Fat Tee was tempted to run upstairs and get a few more of the diamonds. But to do so would give away his edge. He remembered the promise he'd made to himself about being patient.

"Like I said, I can get more, but you're going to have to give me twenty-four hours, no more than forty-eight, to get 'em here," he said.

"Too bad," said Bone, his hand snaking around to the back of his waistband. The reptilian hand returned, holding a black Glock. "Don't think I'm going to be able to wait that long. Frankly, I ain't got that type of time to waste on you."

Bone put the four bogus bankrolls—cut-up newspaper with hundreds on the top and bottom of each stack—back in his bag, along with the diamonds. When he zipped it, to Fat Tee's ears it sounded like a body bag being closed.

"What's taking you so long, bee?" Bone pointed the nasty end of the Glock at Fat Tee's jewels, his *other* jewels. Fat Tee cringed involuntarily. "I told you that I didn't have all day, didn't I? Now turn your pockets out like rabbit ears. Let me see what else you holding." Bone was as calm as he was composed. The way the ocean is before the storm.

With options as tight as the eyes of a drunken Chinese man, Fat Tee ran his pockets. They were empty except for a few bills: three twenties, a ten, and a five—chump change. "This all I got, bee," he said, mirroring Bone's New York vernacular. Fat Tee hated New York niggas. And being stung by one wasn't helping with public relations as far as he was concerned.

A noise coming from the other side of the door caught both Fat Tee and Bone off guard and demanded their attention.

"You expecting someone?" Bone asked. His plan was to put a couple of slugs in Fat Tee's head, using a pillow to muffle the sounds, but the unexpected guest may have put a wrinkle in that plan.

Working with the cards he was dealt, Fat Tee told a lie. "Just another customer." In truth, he was just as baffled as Bone. He wasn't expecting anybody.

Bone held up the bag where he'd put the diamonds and the fake money rolls. "I thought you said these were all the diamonds that you had?" he said suspiciously.

"Wasn't sure if you would buy all three," Fat Tee came back quick, and said with a poker face. "Hell. Wasn't even sure if you would show up, bee. Not like we've ever did any type of . . ." His words trailed off as his eyes focused on the gun in Bone's hand, his mouth dryer than a five-dollar-hoe's pussy.

"Not like we ever done any type of business before," he finished.

Whoever was at the door hadn't knocked, but the shadow from their feet could be seen through the crack at the bottom. Four feet. The math was simple. At least two people were out there, and nine times out of ten it wasn't the Girl Scouts attempting to sell their Thin Mints cookies.

Fat Tee could tell that Bone was contemplating what to do. Improvisation had gotten many men killed, and even more locked up, when the wrong move was made.

Bone made up his mind. He said, "Lay facedown on the bed!"

Fat Tee, fearing the outcome of Bone's plan stood statue still.

"Don't make me ask you twice, bee!" Bone pushed Fat Tee toward the bed. "Now put that pillow over your head and count to a hundred."

A NASCAR engine would have had trouble keeping up with the pace of Fat Tee's heart rate when the pillow blocked out the light. Fearing that he would never see the light of day again, Fat Tee almost pissed on himself. One . . . two . . . three . . .

Bone rummaged through the drawers on the dresser and the armoire.

"Eight . . . nine . . . ten . . ."

He heard the door to the fridge open.

"Sixteen . . . seventeen . . . eighteen . . ."

Then he heard a sound that he wasn't expecting but he was grateful he did. The window squeaked from years of neglect. He heard boots clanging against the metal. Bone made his way down the fire escape.

Thirty-nine . . . forty . . . forty-one . . . forty-two . . . forty-three . . .

Fat Tee opened his eyes. He hated New York niggas.

Fuck them bitches. GOD, if I live I'm packing up and getting the fuck outta here! But what the fuck and why the fuck I let this bitch keep putting me in these situations?

FIVE DAYS EARLIER . . .

The elevator doors glided open on the twenty-sixth floor. Dapper, charismatic, handsome Kennard DuVall was dressed as sharp as a tack as he stepped out of the metal box onto the plushy carpeted hallway with his Presidential Suite keycard in hand and an enormous smile on his face. As he strolled down the hallway, he had every right in the world to be high on life: In a few hours, he was about to pull off promoting the biggest boxing match of the decade and it was going down in New York City, his hometown. Madison Square Garden had already sold out months ago, the Pay-Per-View numbers were record-breaking and like water, the money was pouring in like the floodgates had been broken down. Not to mention the star power and media that had come into town to either cover or witness the bout between Taymar Woodley and Jockney Jang, two of the most controversial boxers of modern days.

All was magnificent in Kennard's world. His money

was right, his love life was tight, and in about six months, he was going to be a daddy. His best friend and love of his life, Unique, was expecting their first child. That last thought carved a colossal grin into his face. He felt like a jack-o'-lantern that had just gotten lit up. In his mind, finding Unique was like finding a needle in a haystack, good karma, or something one of the gods had sent to him. She was everything any man could want. Drop-dead gorgeous, she had a beautiful personality, and was giving, caring, honest, loyal, a freak in the bed, and built like a superhero.

In front of the suite, Kennard paused. He put his ear to the door. It was a habit he'd picked up a long time ago. Though he completely trusted Unique, he never liked surprises. He couldn't remember what time Unique had mentioned that her glam squad would be there to get her all dolled up for the fight. He didn't think she really needed the makeup artist or hairstylist anyway; she was already a doll from the get-go. However, he understood the type of girl she was. She looked like a beauty from a Cover Girl commercial from the moment he met her and had maintained that same image throughout their relationship. He knew that she always wanted to look her absolute best for *him* and to represent *him* in the finest way possible, so he just rolled with the punches and bankrolled all the costs. From the other side of the double doors, all he heard was silence, so he was certain he could get a few minutes of alone time with his girl.

He wasn't known to be a trick-ass dude, and wasn't in the business of taking care of women, but Unique was different. She genuinely strived to make him happy—however, whenever. She always put him first, making him her priority, and for that alone, he was happy to provide her with anything her heart desired.

Down the hall, a woman got off the elevator and gave him a hard, strange look. She probably took him for a jealous husband, a thief, or even worse, a pervert. A little embarrassed, Kennard straightened up and removed his ear from the door before the chick's curiosity drove her to call security, a hassle he didn't need. Hell, he'd booked the majority of the rooms on his floor, plus suites on three other floors in the hotel as comps for boxers, their entourage and families, and his VIPs attending the fight. Kennard shot her a this-is-my-room look, and then sheepishly shoved his key-card down the mouth of the automatic lock. The light turned from red to green.

The Presidential Suite was as opulent as it was huge. A white baby grand piano was the focal point of the room. He smiled, thinking there was something about a baby grand piano that represented class and wondered about the people who had occupied the room before him, who actually played. Baby grands sat in many living rooms of the wealthy and upper class without a single soul in the dwelling even knowing how to play one note of "Mary Had a Little Lamb."

A long dining-room table was off to the left and comfortably seated sixteen, and a sofa and loveseat were arranged around a gas fireplace that had a fifty-inch flat-screen TV over it. There were four bedrooms, two on each side, and Kennard headed toward the master bedroom, which was on the far right of the suite.

Once inside, Kennard could hear the shower running in the bathroom. He knew Unique wasn't expecting him. She had been so great about understanding how busy he was this week and not being on his heels, but keeping herself available when he needed her. They were supposed to meet downstairs later for pictures and then head out to the fight, but he knew she'd be delighted that he had found some extra time and decided to spend it with her.

Kennard felt bad about all the time he'd spent away from her over the past few weeks. Prior to this fight, they had spent a lot of quality time together, but he planned to make it up to her after the event was over. He was going to surprise her with a trip to Paris. Just the two of them—no assistants, no glam squad, no work, but plenty of play and monster shopping in the city of love. He'd already bought the plane tickets and had everything planned. He wanted to travel and to give her a good time before her belly started to show. Plus, travel would get harder, the further she was along.

He took off his suit jacket and thought about waiting until she got out of the shower, to surprise her. But then he remembered how long her showers usually were and changed his mind. He also didn't have that long before duty would call. He tossed his Armani jacket onto the chair in front of the bed. If he hurried, he could join her for a *quickie* shower.

Unique called it Aqua Sex. Sir Nose, a member of the classic group, Parliament, coined it Aqua Boogie. Kennard sang the lyrics to the old song as he turned the knob. "Aqua boogie . . . under water, doing it just for you-ou."

When Kennard saw Unique sprawled out on the floor, he thought she had fallen and bumped her head. "Baby!" he called out, rushing over to her. But as he bent down to try to help her up, the blood and the bruises on her body quickly dispelled that belief.

"Unique!"

The shower water had overflowed and mixed with Unique's blood, creating a crimson river all across the floor.

"Shit! Baby!"

Kennard fell to his knees by Unique's side. "God, no." If she was breathing at all, he couldn't tell. He didn't want to acknowledge that judging from the circumstances, Unique's odds of living weren't good but the thing he did know was that Unique was used to beating the odds. He prayed that she at least had enough strength still left inside of her to fight now.

"Baby, just hang in there for me. Please, baby." He prayed that she heard him. "I'm here, baby." He got no response from her.

"Who did this to you, baby?" His words echoed off the walls. He felt her neck for a pulse but there was none. He wanted her to answer him because it went without saying that whoever did this was going to pay. That wasn't a threat. It was a promise on everything he loved.

Kennard felt like he was having an out-of-body experience. The room started spinning slowly at first, then picked up speed. He felt a pain in his chest, like his breast plate had been cut open with the jagged edges of a broken Hennessy bottle by a blind surgeon who had had way too much to drink. He could feel a hand squeezing his heart until it was unable to pump the needed blood to other parts of his body. He felt numb, confused, sad, and angry all at the same time. His emotions were running wild.

He gave himself a mental pimp slap across the face and ordered himself to tighten the fuck up. This was not the time to lose it. He had seen blood before and had even inflicted wounds on men that produced more blood than this, so this wasn't new to him.

Kennard inhaled deeply, the way he used to calm himself down when he was in the boxing ring. More often than not, the technique usually helped him regain his composure. This time was a little different—it helped some but not so much.

Kennard knew that he had to get her immediate medical attention, but he didn't want to leave Unique's side. It was like a lightbulb went off in his head when he remembered that his cell phone was in his pocket and dialed for help.

"Nine-one-one, what's your emergency?" the operator said.

The woman's voice sounded jaded. As if she would have rather been somewhere else, doing anything besides what she was doing. That made three of them; he was sure that Unique didn't want to be there in this condition, either. At least the operator was getting paid, was conscious, and didn't have the unconscious love of her life in her arms.

He said, "My fiancée has been . . . ," then paused, realizing that he had no idea what had happened to her. "I found her in the bathroom unconscious. Blood is everywhere. She has bruises all over her body like someone attacked her. Send help."

"Sir . . ." the operator asked after a brief pause that

felt like an eternity, "can you tell me where you are calling from?"

He told the operator where he was.

Nonchalantly, she said, "A paramedic is on the way. If you like, you can stay on the line."

Kennard didn't even recall pushing the End button, and disconnecting the line. He grabbed the hotel phone that had been placed in the bathroom and called down to the front desk, where Sheila, the woman on duty, answered, and he briefly explained the situation. Unlike the emergency operator, Sheila wasn't inured to day-to-day fatal crises. Kennard had spoken to her the past couple of days about deliveries, VIP guests, and their wants or needs. His name warranted her attention, but his situation evoked panic in her voice.

"Oh my God!" she exclaimed. "I'm calling EMT right now, Mr. DuVall, as well as sending help up." She mentioned that the hotel had a house doctor—her inflection indicating that she wasn't sure if he would be much help but she said she'd already rung his phone.

Kennard thanked her and hung up, then clung on to Unique's hand and prayed to the Almighty for help.

Looking into Unique's slack face he thought, *This can't be happening again.* The thought wouldn't stop echoing inside his head.

This whole scenario was like someone had pressed

the previous scene button on the DVD of his life. His mind flashed back nine years to when his former pregnant girlfriend, Kyra, had been kidnapped and murdered. He never wanted to experience that hollow feeling again, like his insides were being sucked out of his body, when he had to identify Kyra's body at the morgue. Her body had been mutilated by bullet wounds. The loss was immeasurable and he never thought he would recover.

Now, it was happening all over again, to him, his girl, and their unborn child. This couldn't be his life. He had been living the right way. He wasn't in the streets conducting illegal business anymore. This couldn't be his destiny.

But as sad as it was unfolding, it was!

MADHOUSE

Tyeedah made her way through the opulent lobby of the Tabby Hotel, trying to figure out what the hell all the commotion was about. She had been coming and going in and out of the hotel for the past few days, hanging out with her best friend Unique, and although the place had been a spectacle all week this evening took the cake. It looked like a full-blown circus with bona fide clowns, certified jokers with both famous and wannabe entertainers, ballplayers, security, and groupies, not to mention the paramedics wheeling an empty stretcher through the lobby. If she hadn't been summoned the best seat in the house was in the lobby, people watching.

Tyeedah shook her head at the traveling acts posted up in the lobby, but more so she could not believe how quick the clock was moving. After the massive traffic on the Brooklyn Bridge, she was running about thirty minutes behind schedule and now she had to deal with this.

She pushed her way through the crowd, allowing her oversized overnight bag to lead the way to the elevator bank. "Excuse me," she said firmly to a man that thought he was a statue. "Like, hello, I'm trying to get through to the elevator, please."

He sucked his teeth. "Isn't everybody trying to get upstairs?" he said back to her.

"Yeah, but I'm actually a guest. Now, let me by and stop acting like the Statue of Liberty."

He sucked in his stomach, took a half step to the right, and offered an apology as Tyeedah scooted by.

After navigating the human minefield, she made it to the other side of the lobby. She was happy that the security guard blocking the elevators recognized her and let her get through to the elevators with no problem. Tyeedah pushed one of the buttons that controlled the elevators to the tower she wanted. To her surprise, the six shiny gold-plated doors opened immediately. She stepped in and hit the button that would take her to the twenty-sixth floor.

As soon as the doors closed, she exhaled, knowing good and well that she was going to have to listen to Unique bitch at her for being late. "Girl," she could already hear her best friend's voice in her head, "why the hell you always got to be on CP time?"

And Tyeedah would answer the same as she always did. "Because I *am* a colored person, bitch." Then they both would fall into laughter. That was the beauty of their friendship. They had no problem finding the humor in everything and they accepted each other's flaws—and lateness was definitely one of Tyeedah's shortcomings.

The elevator glided through the shaft without interruption, heading to the twenty-sixth floor. Finally, she was where she needed to be to begin the process of getting glammed up for the fight. Her hair was already in check; it was the makeup and wardrobe that needed to come together. She and Unique had been looking forward to this big night. Unique was excited that the fight would bring lots of success to her man's business and that things would get back to normal with her and Kennard. Tyeedah was excited because she knew Kennard would make sure that Unique and her would have a nice time, along with nicer seats. The ringside seats would give Tyeedah a bird's-eye view of the major players and put her in immediate proximity of them, which was just up her alley. After all, she wasn't the one damn near married. Tyeedah was single and ready to mingle.

The elevator *ding*ed when it reached the penthouse floor. As she stepped off the elevator, disorder was all around her. If the lobby had been a circus, then the twenty-sixth floor was nothing short of a madhouse. Along with guests standing around trying to get an eyeful of whatever had caused the commotion, Tyeedah saw the NYPD, hotel security, and some other toy cops trying to control the parade of nosy folks.

If this place ain't running neck and neck with the Ring-ling Bros. and Barnum & Bailey circus, my name ain't what it is. Hell, if it wasn't a mixed crowd, I would have sworn this place was the UniverSoul Circus. What in the hell is going on here? She thought about stopping so she could give the scoop to Unique. If she came with gossip, then that might excuse her tardiness. Since time was of the essence, she decided to mind her own business and keep it moving to get to where she was supposed to have been thirty-five minutes ago.

However, all the chaos seemed to come from the same direction she was headed. When she rounded the corner, her heart dropped when she realized that all the hoopla was coming from the end of the hall, focusing on suite 2649, the same suite in which her best friend and partner-in-crime was staying.

"What the fuck?" she muttered under her breath. She put the pep in her step and started running toward the room, pushing her way through the throng of people.

She made her way past the bystanders, but was stopped dead in her tracks at the door by an officer of the law. "Sorry, miss, but you can't go in there."

"This is my sister's room," she informed the officer. "Unique Bryant. She's a registered guest in the room."

The cop paused for a second as he wondered if he should let her go. "You have to wait out here, miss."

"What?" Tyeedah almost bit the officer's head off, then she said with some pitch in her voice, "This is my sister's room. I need to get in there."

"I'm sorry, miss." And although the man was only doing his job, Tyeedah immediately disliked him for what he was about to say. "But you're going to have to wait out here until we get the situation under control."

"Situation? What's going on?" She could tell by the look on his face that he wasn't going to give her any more information.

Tyeedah was pretty sure that she could take him. She turned to calmly walk away and just when the officer thought she had let it go, without any notice, she tried to push past him. Not a good idea. He was only a few inches taller than her, but outweighed Tyeedah by about a hundred pounds, mostly around the middle. He easily held her off.

"That was a good attempt, but I can't let you go in there."

"But you can," Tyeedah insisted. "You just won't."

"Look, miss, I can't let you go in there," he said firmly. "I understand you are concerned for your loved

one, but it will help if you wait out here. I cannot let you go in there."

She could tell by the look in his eyes that he meant business, but there were always two ways to skin a cat so she started to scream at the top of her lungs, "Unique! Unique! Kennard! Kennard!" hoping that they were all right and that one if not both of them would hear her making such a ruckus and would tell the officers it was okay to let her in.

She only wanted to know if Unique and Kennard were fine. Maybe it was a break-in, she tried to convince herself. But deep down in her gut, her street smarts knew that the police wouldn't have come out in this type of numbers for a B&E. And there would be no need for paramedics. "Unique . . . Kennard!" she kept calling out, hoping and praying for a response from one of them.

"Miss," said the overweight officer, who was not only holding her back but blocking her view as well, "you're gonna hafta keep it down."

Tyeedah didn't care about him. He wasn't on her side, and she had no use for him. "Fuck you!" She was tired of this fool telling her what she couldn't do. "My sister and brother-in-law may be in there and you're playing these games with me."

Just then her tantrum was interrupted by a loud, clear, firm voice, saying, "We need to clear a path so

that we can get out of here. People, we must clear the way. We have to get to the hospital." The voice had come from inside the suite. The officers in the hall went into action and began clearing a path so that they could get the stretcher out and to the elevators.

Tyeedah's heart almost fell into her pumps when she saw the gurney being pushed by the EMT guys with Unique lying on top. "Oh my God," she said out loud.

Kennard was right alongside the gurney. His clothes were discolored from what appeared to be Unique's blood, but he kept stride with the fast-moving gurney as he held her hand. Tyeedah peered into Unique's eyes. They looked empty. "Kennard," she blurted out as he and the two emergency technicians rolled past her. "What happened to her?"

Kennard didn't answer. He seemed to have a one-track mind. He walked right past as if he didn't even see her.

"Kennard, tell me what happened to my sister." When he still didn't answer, Tyeedah thought that Kennard might be in shock and so tongue-tied that he couldn't even answer.

The sea of onlookers that filled the hall parted as the gurney made its way to the elevator.

"Kennard, that's my sister! What happened to her?" she asked with eyes and a tone that demanded an answer.

An officer tried to stop Tyeedah from getting on. Kennard looked at him and said, "Let her on." Tyeedah slid her body through the elevator doors just as they were closing.

It hurt her to see her friend like that. Unique had been so full of life, and seeing her almost lifeless body and the harm that had been inflicted on her brought tears to Tyeedah's eyes.

Kennard got the words out. "I don't know what happened. She was attacked, brutally beaten and left for dead. I came back to the room to try to get a little time with her before y'all showed up and found her lying on the bathroom floor with no pulse or anything."

Tyeedah believed him. Fire, hurt, pain, and anger were written all over his face.

The elevator seemed to fly down to the lobby, as if it could also sense the urgency. As soon as the door popped opened, the wheels of the gurney were gliding across the marble floor of the lobby of the Tabby Hotel, then out the door to the waiting ambulance.

With Kennard on one side and Tyeedah on the other, they were there every step of the way until Unique was put into the back of the ambulance and Kennard got in with her. When the doors were about to shut, Tyeedah asked, "What hospital y'all taking her to?"

"Mount Sinai."

The trained driver of the emergency vehicle was no slouch. He pulled that ambulance into New York City traffic and peeled out like he was a NASCAR driver.

KEYLESS IN THE
UNITED STATES OF AMERICA

In the coffee shop across the street from the hotel, Fat Tee sat nervously sipping on an espresso, looking out the window at the front entrance of the Tabby Hotel. He couldn't stop replaying how he had finagled his way into the hotel's Presidential Suite less than an hour ago when he posed as Kennard.

He had to admit he was a genius and deserved a pat on his back to be able to pull that stunt off. It went to show that any hotel can be broken into. His momma always told him, if he believed, he would achieve.

By luck Fat Tee saw that a room service attendant had left the service elevator unattended and while no one was looking, he hopped on and took it straight to the penthouse floor.

"Excuse me, miss," he said to the housekeeper who was vacuuming with her headphones on.

The housekeeper never looked up from her work. Her mind seemed to be a thousand miles away, oblivious to her surroundings.

Fat Tee spoke up and said again, "Excuse me, miss!" He waved his hand in her line of vision. Her hand snapped up and her eyes showed embarrassment and guilt that she was not being attentive to one of her valued guests. She quickly cut off the vacuum cleaner and said, "Pardon me. Me no see you here, sir." Fat Tee could see the nervousness in her eyes. He could tell that she thought she may be in trouble, and he used that weakness against her.

"Not a problem at all," said Fat Tee, in an attempt to ease her mind and relax her more. "You don't know how glad I am that you're here." As he spoke, he looted his pockets, in search of a key that was never there in the first place.

Lola, the housekeeper, gave him a slight smile and asked, "How may I help you?" The interruption was delaying her from finishing her work but she was glad that he was a nice man and that she wasn't in any trouble.

Fat Tee said, "I'm trying to get into my room. But I must have left my keycard inside."

Lola seemed to ponder his request and she knew it was against the rules for housekeepers to use their master keys to let guests into rooms. After a brief pause, she dropped her head, wishing she could help. "Me so sorry, sir." Not the answer Fat Tee was hoping for. "No allowed to do this."

Fat Tee told her that he understood. "However," he said, not willing to give up that easily, "I really have to use the bathroom." He made faces as if the insides of his stomach were at war. "Very bad."

Lola looked around, unsure of what she should do, hoping someone else would show up to help her decision.

Taking advantage of her indecisiveness, Fat Tee said, "There's no way I can make it to the desk for a replacement key without overloading my drawers." He squeezed his legs as if he was really trying to hold his bowels. Then he lowered his tone as if the two of them were sharing a secret. He leaned in closer and said to her, using his best Southern charm, "I have the runs." By the look on her face, Fat Tee figured that the housekeeper didn't understand what he was saying. He had an idea. "Vroom! Vroom!" With both hands on his butt, he made a squatting motion. "Runs," he said again. "Vroom! I have the runs."

Lola's eyes brightened with recognition of what Fat Tee had been trying to say. Then her normally sand-colored cheeks reddened with embarrassment.

"You sick," she said.

"Me so sick," Fat Tee assured her, nodding his head and somehow he made his eyes water a little like he was so anxious to go. "So you need to let me into my room, or give me a roll of toilet paper so that I can shit

right here, because I have no intentions of dumping my load in my drawers." He paced back and forth three times, then he stopped and crossed his ankles like he was desperate to hold it in. "And I don't think management will appreciate you telling their guest to shit in the hallway." Unsure of how much of what he said the housekeeper understood, Fat Tee started unbuckling his belt as if he was more than prepared to follow through on his threat.

Lola's arm shot out like a traffic monitor trying to cut short an eight-year-old from running into a busy street. "No! No!" she said, begging. "Please. No do that." Digging out the master keycard from her workpants she said, "No vroom-vroom in hall. Come, come. Me let you in room." She was afraid that she would have to clean up the mess and probably get fired for letting someone of caliber use the bathroom on himself. After all, since he was staying in the Presidential Suite, he must be a rich man, but more important, a VIP! Lola swiftly fed the keycard into the lock, unknowingly allowing an intruder into Unique's room.

Inside the room, Fat Tee's intentions, at first, were to tighten Unique up a little for pulling the pistol out on him the previous day. It never dawned on Fat Tee that if he hadn't cornered Unique, demanding that she set Kennard up to be robbed, that she never would have had to threaten him with the gun in the first place.

To him, it didn't matter that he was the one that had cornered her. *Fuck, she thought she was Jessica James or somebody?*

Honestly, once inside the room, Fat Tee hadn't intended for events to unfold the way they did or the shit to go as far as it did. While she was in the shower, he snuck in and cut the lights to scare her and catch her off guard. He yanked her out of the shower and hit her with a blow to the head. At first Unique was off balance, but she was a tough cookie, though, and the whore could take a punch better than some men could. Although the blow took the wind out of her, it didn't take long for her to bounce back. Once Unique bit off his earlobe and snapped her knee up into his crotch like she was trying to place gold in the Tae-Bo Olympics, Fat Tee lost it. At first the pain immobilized him. Writhing in pain, he thought she had gotten out on him again.

He hated that she was still able to inflict pain upon him. Mentally, it was more than he could handle. The way she had played with his emotions so many years ago, the way she not only set him up to be robbed blind, not once but twice. Kicking a man in his private parts was a treacherous pain but killing a man's ego and pride was even worse. No way in this lifetime was he going to let a bitch, a worthless, nothingless, trick-ass-whore-turned-housewife, whip him. With that being said, rage set in and caused him to black out. All he wanted was to make this bitch suffer until her dying breath.

When he set out for New York City a couple of months ago, all Fat Tee had wanted was to be properly compensated for what Unique and her ex-boyfriend, Took, had taken from him. But then as soon as Fat Tee saw that she was living larger than anyone from Virginia had ever expected her to, that quickly changed. He had spent so much energy hating her and blaming her for his misfortunes that he could never focus on trying to pick up the pieces and get money like he always had. His hate for Unique had taken over his life for the past seven years.

He felt she deserved everything he could squeeze out of that raunchy bitch. How did she think she was going to be living the life of luxury in New York City, not thinking twice about him, after he was left in Virginia scrambling? He had never recovered mentally or emotionally from when Took and her had gotten him—and left him for broke. He simply couldn't help or control himself from snapping out on Unique.

When Fat Tee finally came out of his maniac fugue, gaining control of his faculties for the first time, he saw Unique lying on the floor in a crimson pool. She wasn't moving. He kicked her. "Bitch, get up!" he said.

She was nonresponsive, and for a minute he thought

he lying killed her and he was happy if he did. In his eyes, the bitch deserved to die.

"That's what you get, beyatch, for fucking my life up the way you did!" he said as if she could hear him and then he spit on her. But seeing her lying there so helpless and lifeless, for a moment, he sobered up quickly.

"I gotta get the hell outta here," he said out loud. Fat Tee went into the closet and got out a suit that probably belonged to Kennard. He grabbed a plastic hotel-issued laundry bag off another rack and put his bloody clothes inside it. He wiped everything down that he had touched, besides Unique. His eyes scanned the bathroom to be sure he hadn't missed anything. He thought how it looked like a bad scene from a horror movie.

Sneaking out the door in Kennard's suit, Fat Tee thought, *There's always one survivor in those movies, and that's me.*

Two hours later, Fat Tee sat with a bird's-eye view of everything coming and going in and out of the Tabby Hotel. He pretended to read *The New York Times* while sipping on his coffee and watching the fire department arrive first, then the paramedics, and finally the police. From the top speed in which the paramedics were moving, Tee guessed that the damage he had done to Unique wasn't fatal. He smiled to himself, thinking how tough Unique really was—that was the thing he always loved about her, her tenacity.

He sat in in his booth dumbfounded and before he had even realized it, he had mumbled under his breath, "Damn, the beyatch ain't dead after all!"

THE CIRCUS

Tyeedah arrived at the hospital a few minutes after the ambulance. She gave the cabbie a hundred dollars and ran inside, just in time to see two nurses prying Kennard's hands away from Unique to take her into surgery.

Once Unique was taken behind the double doors for the doctors to work wonders on their friend, she hugged Kennard. "She's a fighter. You gotta know she's going to pull through this." She tried to console him though she had tears in her eyes. Tyeedah truly believed what she was saying; she just hoped that God did, too.

It was hard for her, but she knew she had to be strong for her best friend's man. She knew firsthand how much the two of them loved each other.

Together they waited in the designated area for family and friends. It damn near broke Tyeedah's heart when she saw the doctors have to pry Kennard's hands away from Unique's. Though she had heard about Kennard's reputation with the girls around town long before Unique had even stepped foot in the city, having a front-row seat to witness firsthand their relationship develop from the very second it started could only lead to one question in Tyeedah's head.

Tyeedah's mind went back to the one-in-a-million encounter.

The party was in the Hamptons. A rapper who Tyeedah had become pen pals with in prison, invited her. Once they both returned to society, every now and again he came through and hit it. Though there was nothing serious between the two of them, he didn't let the fact that his name was in lights affect anything between them. He still kept it real with her and made sure that Tyeedah's name was on the list.

At first, Unique didn't believe Tyeedah when she informed them of their trip to the Hamptons and claimed that Diddy was throwing the party. But to be honest, she didn't care if that bad boy was being catered by Osama bin Laden, Unique wasn't turning down the opportunity to flaunt her stuff in the Hamptons practically since she arrived in New York. In her eyes it was a hell of a welcoming party.

On that Friday, they got there early to make sure everything was in order. They didn't want to be embarrassed if God forbid their names weren't on the guest list. But not only were they on the guest list as promised, Tyeedah's friend had set them up in VIP.

Standing by the poolside and admiring all the famous guests, Unique had told Tyeedah, "There must not be a concert anywhere in the country tonight, because everybody and their cousin is up in here." Everywhere they looked there was a celebrity.

Chicks were eyeballing the two of them down like they were purple martinis with green boogers. Tyeedah and Unique could never figure out why some girls had a problem complimenting other women since this was so not the case for either of them. In their minds, they may not have had the money or fame that a lot of these chicks had, but they could hold their own in the body and looks department. Giving others their just due was easy when one didn't have insecurities of oneself.

Tyeedah was bothered by how chicks were gritting on them, but Unique was enjoying herself to the fullest. The deejay was spinning on the wheels of steel and Unique started moving her shoulders, swaying her hips and snapping her fingers.

Unique said, "Oh, that's my jam right there!"

Feeling the beat of the music, Unique started shaking what her momma gave her and drawing attention to herself. Just when she was just about ready to show them how to drop it like it was hot, VA style, someone bumped her, spilling some of the drink he was holding in his hand onto her dress.

"What the hell?" She whipped around on five-and-a-half-inch heels, ready to curse out a clumsy, ditsy bitch. The sexy number she was wearing cost a grip and she had not even gotten a good wear out of it.

Unique couldn't believe her eyes. To her surprise, the culprit standing in front of her wasn't at all what she was expecting. To say the least, she was pleasantly surprised. Boy, the big city had her dreaming even bigger.

The hating chick turned out to be a six-foot-three man with the whitest teeth and the darkest, smoothest skin that looked tastier than Godiva chocolate. He had wavy hair, a killer smile, and black diamonds for eyes.

Unique watched his lips as the words rolled off his tongue "My name is Kennard," he said in a way that she would have bet her last piece of cash or ass that "Swagger" was his middle name.

Maybe it was the alcohol but she liked the way his New York accent snapped off each syllable and that voice of his made the hairs on the back of her neck stand up.

She said, "Don't worry about it, hon!" The realness of the matter was that she would let a brother that fine dump a bucket of water on her, and as hot as he was, she would need every drop to cool down.

Those eyes that sparkled like chocolate diamonds looked directly into hers. "At least let me have your dress cleaned. You are wearing it so well I would hate to be responsible for the destruction of such a masterpiece." He shook his head and looked her over. "I wouldn't be able to forgive myself."

She shrugged her shoulders and acted like she had a closet full of designer dresses. "It's nothing." She gave him her sexy voice and best smile. "As long as what's in the dress is okay." She looked up into his glistening eyes. "That's all that matters."

Unique could tell that he was used to women flirting but he seemed to enjoy the sport and most of all, the prelude to what might be.

His stare was hungry, like a lion that hadn't eaten in a week staring at its prey. "From my vantage point, *what's in the dress* is a whole lot better than okay, but I won't take no for an answer."

Looking in his eyes, never showing that she was the least bit confused by what he meant, she asked, "No to what?"

"Dinner? Breakfast? Lunch? New dress?" He turned his hands up toward the stars. "The sky's the limit and I'm not hard to get along with, I just want to get to know you better."

Unique wasn't looking for a quick fuck and was reluctant to accept what he was offering. Those days for her were over. She'd had enough of those to last her a couple of lifetimes. Although Kennard looked like he could really work it, she turned to Tyeedah.

Tyeedah nodded and gave a look that translated to: *Bitch, you better go with him.*

Unique did, and from that moment on, she and Kennard never left each other's side. Nine months later, their love for each other seemed to grow deeper and deeper every day.

And if anybody had ever doubted Kennard's love for Unique, this day was the proof. Together, Tyeedah and Kennard waited in the room designated for family and friends. After about an hour of Kennard pacing the floor, two men in cheap suits and soft bottom, lace-up shoes walked in and approached him.

The taller of the two offered Kennard his hand. "I'm Detective Jones," he said with deference in his tone. "This is my partner, Detective McGeary. Sorry to have to meet like this, Mr. DuVall." The empathy in his voice implied that he didn't want to be there any more than Kennard did. "But we have a few questions that need to be asked."

Kennard's red eyes held Detective Jones's stare.

Forging forward, Detective Jones pulled out a small pad. He checked his personal notes and said, "So you were the one that found Ms. Bryant in the bathroom?"

Kennard nodded.

Detective Jones waited a few beats to be sure Kennard didn't want to elaborate further. Sometimes witnesses and suspects alike would run off at the mouth a mile a minute, unprompted, and sometimes they had to be coerced. "In your own words, can you tell me what happened, from the beginning?"

Like most young black males that grew up in the hood, Kennard wasn't a big fan of the police.

"Do we have to do this now?" Tyeedah interjected.

"Look, sir," Detective Jones said, never acknowledging Tyeedah, "I know this is hard for you."

Detective Jones flipped his hands palms up in a gesture indicating that it didn't matter to him either way, but said, "The quicker we get the information that we need, the quicker we can catch the perp." Jones was a fourteen-year vet with the NYPD and knew how to handle these types of situations. "However," he added, "based on my experience, it's usually best to get this stuff out of the way as soon as possible. While the events are still fresh on the mind."

Kennard sucked in a deep, restorative breath, squared his shoulders, then exhaled. "Okay," he said. "Let's just get this over with. What is it that you need to know?"

"Like I said," said Jones, "I just need to hear your version of what took place."

Your version. Kennard didn't appreciate the words Detective Jones chose to use or the tone in which he said them—as if there was more than one version. Kennard's antenna instantly went up. He knew, from experience, that when something happened to a girl-friend or a spouse, the first person the police looked at was the man in the relationship. Nine years ago, when his baby mother was kidnapped and eventually killed, Kennard had been the main "person of interest" until he provided a plane ticket that put him on a flight back from Vegas at the time in question. Since physics dictated that it was impossible to be in two places at the same time, the police finally backed off.

Not wanting his experiences then to affect the way he interacted with the police now, Kennard swallowed his disdain toward the NYPD's prejudices and for the first time in his life, he shared with the detectives what little he did know. He started with the time he left the hotel room that morning, provided names of most of the people he met with, and how he ended up with some extra time and decided to spend it with his fian-cée. "And that's the way I found her," he said, ending his account.

Detective Jones wrote something down in his pad. "Was there anything—that you know of—missing from the room?"

"I can't say. I wasn't thinking about that type of shit. I'd just found my fiancée lying on the fucking floor in a pool of fucking blood. Didn't think to see if my tie pin was still where I left it."

Ignoring the sarcasm, Jones said he understood.

"But can you tell me if there was anything of value in the room? Something someone would want to take?"

The country was in a recession. What Bernie Madoff didn't steal, people were spending on gas money and food. Of course there were things in the room that someone would steal. But Kennard didn't think there was anything worth beating a woman and leaving her for dead over.

He put his fist over his eyes, trying to knock the image of Unique's battered body from the front of his mind so he could better cope. He said, "Maybe a couple of pieces of jewelry. Nothing serious enough to kill over."

Jones raised a brow as if he was a savant of criminal behavior. "You'd be surprised what people will kill for," he said. "But that's neither here nor there." He seamlessly changed gears.

"What makes you think the perp wanted her dead?" Jones obviously didn't want an answer to that question because he went right on to the next. "Do you know of anyone that may have wanted to do Ms. Bryant harm?"

"If I did," Kennard said straight on, and without reservation, "I'd be already at their asses, not here wasting my time with you." He was getting tired of the Q&A.

"How about you, miss?"

"You speaking to me?" Tyeedah said, surprised

that Detective Jones had directed his line of questioning to her. Up until now he had acted as if she were invisible and not even in the room, which had been fine with her.

"Yeah," Jones said. "Do you know of anyone that may have wanted to hurt Ms. Bryant? Anybody at all?"

Tyeedah thought about the question. She only knew of one person that fit the bill: Fat Tee. He had not only blackmailed and threatened Unique, he had raped her.

"No, I don't," Tyeedah said to the detective.

To link Fat Tee with the crime against Unique meant that Tyeedah would have to give some type of motive. To do so would implicate her and Unique's involvement in a recent diamond heist. There was a time and place for everything, she believed, and *here* and *now* was neither.

Detective Jones eyed his partner, who hadn't said a word since they entered the room. Then he snapped his notepad closed and said, "We'll be in touch."

Neither Kennard nor Tyeedah was sure to whom the detective was referring.

COMA

The next thirty-six hours were torturous for Kennard. That day and a half at the hospital felt more like thirty-six years in a prison cell awaiting execution.

Kennard never left Unique's side and had to be pried away from her before she was taken into surgery. He hated the fact that his actions might have been considered bitch-assness, but Unique was a part of his soul. He didn't give a fuck what it looked like.

The fight at Madison Square Garden took place as scheduled. But he didn't really care about that bout; he and Unique were smack-dab in the middle of their own fight, one with a significantly larger purse: her life.

Unique was now hooked up to a team of lifesaving machines. She was in a coma, and the doctor wasn't sure when or if she would ever wake up. The doctor said that Unique was lucky that Kennard had found her when he did and that the EMT guys had gotten her to the hospital as soon as they did, or she would have died for certain.

With all due respect to the doctor's expertise, Kennard begged to differ. As he looked at his woman lying on a hospital bed, unable to move, Unique didn't appear to be rolling in four-leaf clovers to him. Luck was relative.

Kennard had cleared over eighty million dollars from the fight Saturday night and would have paid every dime of it to be able to change this particular predicament. But it didn't work like that. Shit—life didn't work that way. Money could buy him the best doctors but not time travel or a pass to keep his girlfriend from the gates of heaven or hell for that matter. Regardless of what Disney World wanted people to believe, fantasies didn't accept credit cards.

Kennard had to wrap his head around the reality Unique might never wake up.

The doctor had said that the longer Unique remained with no progress, the more her chances of pulling through decreased.

Kennard wanted to—he so badly needed to—take his anger out on someone, mainly the person or people behind not only this brutal crime to his woman but also of the violation and disrespect to him. Besides wanting Unique to pull through, he wanted to make these horrible people feel her pain and their loved ones to feel his.

He couldn't believe that fate would have it that he

had been in a situation similar to this one, almost a decade ago regarding Kyra, who was then his girlfriend and who, just like Unique, happened to be pregnant with his baby when she was kidnapped and held for ransom.

It didn't matter who did this or how long it would take him to find the people responsible. It had taken him two years of keeping his ear to the streets to find out who had killed Kyra. The murderers turned out to be three cats from Queens, who were delivered to him on a silver platter.

The murderous secret eventually proved to be like water, too hard for them to hold. One of them, a kid name Righteous, started bragging to some homies and it didn't take long for the word to get back to Harlem and straight to Kennard.

Righteous had no problem killing, it seemed—that was easy for him—but he was less keen on pain being inflicted upon him.

A couple of fingers cut off with a reciprocating saw and Kennard and his team weren't able to shut him up. Righteous tried to confess to every abject thing he'd ever done in his miserable life. He would have done anything to stop the pain. Anything to stay alive. He was a real sucker, and he took the coward's way out.

He hadn't given a damn about the pain that had

been inflicted upon Kyra or the hurt Kennard had felt every day afterward.

Kennard only wanted to know two things from Righteous: who were his accomplices and why did they do it?

In return, Kennard promised Righteous that he would not kill him slow . . .

Righteous did not hesitate. He quickly gave up his two cohorts, their names, addresses, birthdays, and shoe sizes. He held back nothing.

When he finished, Kennard thanked him, then shot him in the forehead.

If nothing else, Kennard was a man of his word. As for how Righteous's partners paid for what they had done, that's a whole other story.

Since then he never thought that he would ever love again or find anybody else that he would give his heart to—that was, until the day he innocently bumped into Unique at a party in the Hamptons.

FRESH AND CLEAN

Kennard was brought out of his thoughts of the past by someone calling his name.

"Kennard," the voice was soft. "Wake up."

He jumped, startled. His first thought was that Unique had come out of the deep sleep and had gotten enough strength to speak while he had fallen asleep. He snatched his eyes open so fast the wind from his fanning lashes almost blew a cup off the table.

"You should go down the hall and shower and clean up," the voice said. "Change clothes."

It was Tyeedah. She looked genuinely concerned, both for him and Unique.

Besides his parents, no one had been by his and Unique's side during this crisis like Tyeedah. Kennard didn't really know Tyeedah all that well before this whole ordeal, except that Unique had moved to New York to stay with Tyeedah and that they were aces, but now he knew that it was more than that. Their friendship trumped most others.

Kennard's mother, Ms. Katie, interrupted, "I brought him some nice clean clothes and asked him to go change, but he wouldn't. He has his mind set on being by her side. And if you know anything about my Kennard, you know that once his mind is set, there's no turning back."

Tyeedah took into consideration what his mother said but still tried to convince him. "Look, I can respect you wanting to be here, but trust me: Unique would appreciate it more if you go hit the shower. Blood is not a fresh smell, my brother."

He didn't speak, but he heard her.

"Unique's gonna pull through this sooner rather than later and when she does, you need to have your shit together. And can I have at least thirty minutes to say that I was by her side, please?" She gave him a slight smile. "It don't make no sense how you hogging her bedside from other people who love her, too."

She knew she was getting to him.

"Now go ahead and shower, shave, and shit; I got this," Tyeedah urged Kennard.

He said, "I'm good. But it would be fucked up if I wasn't here when and if she woke up."

By the look in her eyes, he could tell that she understood.

"Well, first, I know more than you. Unique is a fighter and she *will* wake up. And *when* she does, you don't look all that good. In fact . . ." she said, "you look a mess."

Kennard usually was very conscious about his appearance and took notice of himself for the first time since the ordeal. He couldn't help but note his wrinkled clothes had been saturated with blood, and that he smelled. The last thing he wanted was to be mistaken for a crackhead or a bum.

"You don't want to scare the poor girl to death when she wakes up, do you?" She flashed a quick smile. "Let me take the watch for now. You go clean, then get back down here as soon as you can." Tyeedah's eyes went over to Unique and softened more than they already were, before turning back to Kennard. "If she so much as makes a peep while you're gone, I'll call you immediately. Promise."

There were a few things that needed his attention. For one, he needed to put word on the streets that it will be very beneficial by way of a reward for the person that led him to whoever was responsible for this.

He got a whiff of his body odor and thought to himself, *A change of clothes and a shower wasn't such a bad idea, either.*

"You promise to call?"

"So much as a peep," she said. "Now get outta here."

OMG!

No sooner than twenty minutes after Kennard returned, Tyeedah screamed, *"Oh, my God!"*

Kennard was about to turn his attention to Tyeedah to ask her what was wrong when he witnessed the miracle that made her shout out. He wanted to do the same thing when he saw what she was looking at. He wanted to yell at the top of his lungs thanking his Higher Power for not turning His back on him.

Unique was awake. His sleeping beauty had risen from her slumber.

Standing over her, Kennard said, "Baby, welcome back."

Her mouth was dry and sticky and felt like she'd been drinking Elmer's glue. Her body ached like it had been run over by a Mack truck.

For a few minutes, she looked around to place her surroundings and then asked, "Welcome back to where?" Her voice felt scratchy.

"Welcome back to us," Kennard told her. "You have been in a coma for the past day and a half."

Unique had no idea she'd been asleep that long. It felt like she'd only taken a nap.

"Are you okay?" Unique asked.

Kennard nodded. "Yeah, baby. You're the one we're concerned about."

Unique didn't remember anything after preparing for the interviews and pictures that had been lined up the day of the fight. From that point her mind was totally blank, like a memory disk that got too close to a magnet.

Tyeedah said, "It's true," as if she could read her mind.

This was so weird, she thought. "I need some water. It feels like tumbleweeds are in my mouth."

Kennard and Tyeedah gave a small chuckle while Kennard jumped to pour a cup of water from the pitcher that was sitting on the bedside table. He put a straw in the cup and pushed the button on the bed to raise Unique's head and then placed the end of the straw into her mouth. Unique could have held the cup herself, but the care and attention Kennard was giving her felt good.

She took a long pull.

The water was warm, room temperature, and felt

like a much-needed rain shower in the middle of the barren desert. The way a flower must feel when it had been neglected, then finally given a drink before the petals turned completely brittle.

After another sip, this one shorter, she said, "If today is Monday who won the fight?"

Kennard smiled.

"Taymar knocked Jockey out in the sixth round so they tell me, but the fight isn't even important right now, baby. I'm glad that you are awake."

Kennard kissed her lips.

"Don't you remember what happened?" Tyeedah asked. She and Unique locked eyes. Tyeedah looked worried about something.

Kennard interjected, "I found you lying on the bathroom floor. You were . . ." He stopped midsentence and looked like he wanted to spit out more, but instead, swallowed his words.

She could tell from the way his eyes shifted that Kennard was holding something back. He probably thought he was protecting her somehow. He was so unselfish. She wished that she could be more like him.

It was her selfishness, she knew, somehow, that had caused what happened to her like the snowball that caused the avalanche. She knew that much, but the details were still hazy.

Slowly, Unique's memory began to return. In her mind, she was back at the Tabby.

The hotel room, the shower—it was all coming back to her now. Then the lights went out. She had thought it was Kennard playing around.

"Are you okay, babe?" Kennard's voice snapped her thoughts from the hotel room to the hospital room. "You look sorta funny."

"I'm . . . I'm fine. Just trying to remember what happened," she said, sounding like some chick straight out of a soap opera scene. She couldn't believe this type of thing was real. That this was her life and not her favorite characters on *The Young and the Restless* who woke up in hospitals not able to remember how it was they had gotten there.

Kennard rubbed her hair and said, "Don't rush. It will all come back to you soon enough. No need to overwhelm yourself all at once."

It was sound advice, but her mind was running its own show at that moment. It wasn't used to following outside instructions on how to handle inside business. It continued to run the clips from the horrific incident.

She put her hand on her stomach. "The baby?" she questioned. "Is the baby okay?" But by the look in Kennard's eyes, she knew that it wasn't. Tears formed in her eyes. The fact that she had lost the one thing that truly would belong to her and Kennard made the tears turn into sobs.

"Baby, don't worry. Everything is gonna be all right, I promise!" Kennard sealed the promise with a kiss on her forehead.

$$$$$

Once Unique was out of the clear and moved to the Intensive Care Unit, Kennard's parents visited with her. Plus, Detectives Jones and McGeary returned. They wanted to talk to Unique but Kennard stopped them in their tracks. "Look, she just woke up. Let her recover." He tried to be diplomatic.

Tyeedah spoke up. "Look, the bottom line is take that shit to the streets. She can't tell you nothing, 'cause she's still trying to figure out where the hell she is at and who is the damn president."

"Well, miss, we have a job to do and she will need to talk to us now," Detective Jones said.

"Give me your card and I will make sure that she calls you when she is feeling up to it," Tyeedah countered.

Kennard quietly watched as Tyeedah dealt with the police officers.

He listened to Tyeedah and admired the fact that she was really down for Unique. Kennard's daddy used to tell him that there were two types of friends: fair-weather and true. "When things got cloudy the difference would start to surface," his daddy would say, "and when the sky opened, pouring out an all-shit storm and there was only room for one under the umbrella, the one standing there beside you with shit on their face is a true friend."

Kennard could tell that Tyeedah was the type that would stand there with feces covering her face.

"Miss, I know this is a critical time right now," Detective Jones said, although it didn't stop him from his line of questioning, "but do you know anybody who might have wanted to hurt Ms. Bryant?"

Tyeedah paused for a second, ready to cuss him out, but Ms. Katie, Kennard's mother answered instead, in her loving, concerned motherly voice. "That girl was a godsend to my son. She didn't bother a soul and wouldn't want to even hurt a fly."

"So maybe this was random?" Bernard, Kennard's father chimed in.

"Oh, I'm not sure about that, because it looks like a crime of passion," Detective McGeary said.

Detective Jones pulled Tyeedah to the side out of earshot of Ms. Katie and her sanctified friend, but Kennard could still hear. "Was she carrying on an affair with anybody?"

"Are you serious?" Tyeedah asked, then answered,

"No, she was devoted to that man, and they are both madly in love. That's it, that's all."

"So, you don't know anyone who would want to hurt her?"

"Man, what the hell did I tell you already? You fishing in the wrong pond here."

That's what Tyeedah said to the police officer but she knew different and Kennard was going to get to the bottom of it.

POP GOES THE WEASEL

Two hours after the police had left, Tyeedah found herself standing in front of the main entrance to the hospital, watching as the sun reflected off of the skyscrapers. She was ready to call it a day, while inside of her being, optimism, misery, and hopelessness shared the same space. She thought back to her conversation with Kennard that took place moments ago and things were not sitting right with her.

Tyeedah was mad, angry, and just like Kennard, altogether emotionally fucked up. It was one thing not ratting her girl out to the police or her man, but Tyeedah refused to stand around doing nothing while the idiot responsible for putting her friend in an emergency operating room ran around as if everything was all good. *Awww hell no!* She tapped her foot, about to get a whole other attitude at Fat Tee.

It was graveyard quiet since the police had left and Kennard was right beside Unique's bed in the corner of the room facing the door. Tyeedah, sensing he wanted to be alone, had let him marinate in his own mental anguish. Until she couldn't take it anymore, she knew that she had to act.

She spoke softly in a tone right above a whisper as Unique slept. "I have to leave." Kennard was standing in a corner, but his mind was surely in another place. "I'm sorry, but there's something that needs my immediate attention. It just can't be put off any longer."

Unique had called the Big Apple home for less than a year and she didn't have any family in New York. Besides a few acquaintances at culinary school, Tyeedah and Kennard were her only real friends. All the family she had, and Tyeedah felt terrible for having to temporarily run out on her.

Kennard's face was a mask of agony and anger. His eyes—twin volcanoes, bubbling just below the surface, capable of erupting at any provocation—met Tyeedah's as he thanked her for coming. "I'm just really appreciative of you showing up and being here and being her friend."

"No thanks ever needed. I love that girl! I will ride with her until the wheels fall off."

There was nothing else left for either one to say.

His grief was palpable. Unique was the mother of his unborn child. His fiancée. His best friend. And until retribution was exacted upon the person responsible for the pain that was brought upon his family, the healing couldn't begin—neither his nor Unique's. Kennard was not the forgiving type. God forgave freely; but Kennard didn't.

Watching the pain simmering in his eyes, Tyeedah wanted to tell Kennard that she knew how he felt, that she understood the myriad of emotions fighting for supremacy in his head: guilt, sorrow, vengeance, and anguish. She knew that a powerful man rendered powerless over any situation felt less than a man.

Not knowing what else to do, Tyeedah wrapped her arms around him and squeezed him as tightly as she could. She tried to force his pain away with that hug, hoping and praying that she could comfort him the way a sister would console a brother, a mother would her son. In her embrace, Kennard's muscles were so tight, his body felt like a steel beam: hard, cold, unyielding, not reciprocating.

After breaking her hold she said, "Let her know that I'll be back as soon as I'm done. You gonna be okay?"

Kennard nodded. His voice was low and haunting. "I'm a little fucked up right now, but nothing I can't handle." He sounded like Clint Eastwood in one of those old westerns where Clint kills all the bad guys, leaving their bodies stretched out in the middle of a dirty street of a dusty town, not giving a fuck about witnesses.

Honk. Honk.

The horn from a green 2007 Taurus with a dent on the passenger-side door snatched Tyeedah from her thoughts. The driver double-parked as Tyeedah walked toward the car and got in. The door was barely closed when she asked, "What took you so long?"

"Traffic's a bitch," her brother said as a silver Honda Prelude slammed on its brakes to keep from ramming into the back of the Taurus. The driver of the Honda, an old Caucasian lady who resembled Betty White, leaned on the horn. Lil-Bro showed the irate "Senior Citizen Gone Wild" the finger and then he asked his sister, "Where to?" before pulling off.

Tyeedah ignored Lil-Bro's question, asking one of her own. "You got your pistol?"

"Does Hugh Hefner have a lifetime supply of Viagra?"

Taking shots at the oldest playboy in California and his playmates was something they'd always done in the past. Nobody told a dirty joke better than Tyeedah. Lil-Bro, whose real name was Mark, smiled at his mediocre attempt at lightening the moment. Bereft of levity, Tyeedah failed to crack a smirk.

Instead, Tyeedah answered her brother's initial question. "We're going to the Bronx." After she and Unique had robbed the courier for the diamonds to pay blackmail money to Fat Tee, Tyeedah recalled Fat

Tee mentioning where he had been staying because he didn't want to stray far from his motel when he was going to meet the girls to get the diamonds. He was so eager to get his hands on the million dollars he demanded, Fat Tee had been careless. "We're going to Bugley's Inn. But I'm not sure where it is, except that it's near the stadium."

Lil-Bro cut his eye at his sister. When Tyeedah had called him to pick her up from the hospital she didn't give an explanation, nor was one asked or needed for that matter. Lil-Bro loved his older sister unconditionally, more than life itself, and would do anything for her. After all he played a key role in the heist, taking the diamond courier down so that the girls were able to steal the jewels. He owed her that. When Tyeedah was fifteen and Mark ten, their mother OD'd on some bad dope. On the day their mother left this earth to go wherever it was that drug-shooting, bad parents went to when they passed away, Tyeedah promised her brother that she wouldn't let the state of New York take them away. She didn't care what she had to do, she wouldn't allow anyone to come and split them up. She would do whatever was necessary. It wasn't always pretty, but Tyeedah kept her promise. Lil-Bro loved her for it.

Bugley's Inn was a hostel near Yankee Stadium. It was mostly used by prostitutes to turn their hourly tricks and a sprinkling of crack and heroin distributors.

Back in the day, Mark off and on fucked with a chick from that neighborhood, her brother used to brag about all the money he made out of Bugley's Inn selling crack.

Lil-Bro said, "I know where Bugley's Inn is."

"Cool." At least they wouldn't have to waste time searching for a building. A bullet in the head of Fat Tee wouldn't make Unique better, but it was a damn good start.

SPILLING HER GUTS

Two days after Unique became coherent, the doctor released her from the hospital. He told her to take it easy for a while and that time would heal the wounds and that everything would be just fine. It was easy for him to say; he hadn't lost a baby or had a secret to get off of his chest, Unique thought as she sat up in the king-sized bed of the New Jersey home she shared with Kennard.

Kennard walked in just as she was trying to get up. "Where do you think you're going?"

"I was going to try to make me some soup."

"I'm warming up the soup my mom made for you. It'll be ready in a few minutes."

"Thanks, babe," she said.

"Just get back in the bed and remember that the doctor said you gotta take it easy," he reminded her.

"That's easy for him to say, he didn't lose his baby."

Though Kennard had taken it hard, he tried to act like it was all good. "We will make another one. The fun part is making another one." He kissed her on the forehead, trying to reassure her that everything would be okay.

After she finished her soup, she was still sitting up in the bed. He noticed that she had a strange look on her face. "What's wrong, baby?"

"Just a lot on my mind that's all."

"Well, don't let anything worry your pretty little heart. None of this was your fault and everything will be okay."

She took a deep breath. "All of this is my fault."

Kennard immediately tried to shut her down.

"Babe, listen, it's something I have to tell you."

He covered her lips. "Don't worry," he said as he kissed her.

She spoke up, "Listen, babe, I need to tell you something."

"Tell me how much you love me."

"And without a doubt, I do with all my heart." The words came out of her mouth but she allowed her eyes to convey the love she had before she inhaled and continue to speak, "I don't know how to say this."

He finally was getting the message and could see that she had something heavy on her mind. So he just held her hand and listened as she continued, "Baby, I want to say first of all, I love you and I've never loved and trusted anyone more. But the truth of the matter is, there are some things in my past that I'm not proud of."

"And there are some things in my past . . . everybody has skeletons in their closets," he said.

"Yes, but it seems like I have a cemetery." She took in more air and a sip of her juice from the night table. "I know I shouldn't tell you this but I can't hide it from you anymore."

"Hide what?"

"My checkered past. Let me just get it off my chest." She was quiet for a second and then she kept going. "On the bus ride here to New York, I prayed and I prayed, asking God to allow me the opportunity to turn over a new leaf. And funny how he works—because about a week after I arrived, I literally ran into you."

"Yes, I've been known to be a godsend."

"Literally, you were. You brought out the absolute best in me and every day I was with you, I wanted to bury the old me deeper and deeper. And I had done a great job until"—Kennard was looking at her and could see the pain and frustration written all over her face—"until a couple of months ago. It's like one day I walked into the kitchen and my skeletons were all over the kitchen table."

"Okay, I'm a smart guy and am usually quick on my feet, but I'm not following."

By now she was shaking, but holding it all in

wasn't an option anymore. A secret got heavier and heavier the longer it was in tow.

Kennard grabbed her and hugged her. Once he embraced her, her tears became uncontrollable. "Baby, it's okay. Whatever it is, you gonna be okay."

She wiped her tears because she believed him. "I know," she said, "that's the thing. You make me feel so safe, safe to cry and emotionally and physically safe."

Kennard was a bit puzzled. "Who do you fear? Baby, you don't have to be afraid of anyone."

"I'm not really, but know I'm not safe or wasn't ever safe with certain individuals."

"Like who?" Kennard wanted to hear this because anybody who thought they could fuck with anyone he loved had another thing coming to them.

"Baby, I've had a hard life. The only other person I loved or real boyfriend I had besides you was this guy Took, who I cared for deeply. In a nutshell, when he went to jail, I spent his money, then was put in a situation to fend for myself. Everything went to hell, and he never forgave me."

"Is this the motherfucker that did this shit to you?" She could see fire in his eyes.

"No, babe. On another note though, I was set up for some wild shit I didn't even do and sent to prison. Once Took came home from jail, he got me out of that bind. He told me that he used all of his money to get me out and needed to get back on his feet. Now, the old Unique would have never told you this next part, but I'm not her anymore. And besides, if I'm going to have a life with you, I have to be straight with you."

"Agreed," he said, nodding.

"I felt guilty that he spent his last money on me, in spite of the way I was living when he was in. And all I wanted to do was to show him my love, appreciation, and dedication to him and to make our relationship work." She sighed and then said, "I only wanted to prove my love to him."

"So what did you do?"

She was quiet for a beat, wishing that she had not even started pouring her heart and past out to him, but she did and there was only one way to go: forward. "To help him get his money up, he had me line up guys to get robbed."

He was quiet. "So you were a real ride-or-die chick, huh?" he asked in a sarcastic way. "And whatever happened to this Took guy? Are you still in touch with him?"

"I haven't seen him since right after our biggest and last score, when he drugged me, took my passport, and when I woke up, I discovered he'd sold me to a whorehouse in Mexico."

"What the fuc—" Now *that* caught him off guard.

"Our getting back together was all an act for him, and that was his plan the whole time."

"So how did you get out of the whorehouse?" he asked.

"This guy name Lootchee bought me out. I will fill you in on that later. But one of the guys we had robbed was named Fat Tee."

Kennard was listening attentively to everything Unique said.

"Well, he showed and was trying to extort me for money. And to get him the money, I had to rob your jeweler to get the diamonds to pay him."

"You did that?"

Shamefully, she nodded. "Me and Tyeedah did it with the help of her brother."

"Damn."

"I apologize for robbing Shummi and most of all for not telling you these things. I feel bad. I truly do."

"Why didn't you come to me?" He didn't understand.

"I didn't know what to say. What was I going to say? 'Hey, honey, I'm being extorted by someone I set up a long time ago to get robbed and they want a million dollars'?"

"And so where are the diamonds?"

"Fat Tee has them but then he came back, wanting me to set you up to be robbed. Instead, I pulled a gun out on him, and now I know better—I should've shot him. I was taught that if you pull out a gun on some-body you use it."

Kennard had a confused look on his face before he asked, "When did you pull a gun out on him and where was I when all this was going on?"

"Well, it was during the press conference, in the ladies' bathroom in the hotel lobby."

"Damn, I can't believe my security didn't see it hap-pening."

"They did. They caught the tail end of it."

Unique could see the disappointment all over his face and she started to beat herself up inside. If she had only confided in him from the beginning things may have turned out differently. Hell, Fat Tee may have run away and never been heard from again.

There was a minute of silence between the two of them, and after she told him everything, of how Fat Tee had first broken into their home and then how he later assaulted her in the suite, he said one thing, "Trust me. I will take care of everything."

And if she had learned any lesson at all from ev-erything that had happened, she knew that the best thing she could do was trust him.

ROGER THAT

Raindrops—in a rhythm that could've been the track to the next hot summer hip-hop anthem—banged against the windowpane, while gray skies hugged the city like another slow love song.

With Unique asleep in their bedroom, Kennard sat at the desk in the adjoining study, halfheartedly going over a few important papers that he'd been neglecting. He hadn't set foot in his office since last Thursday. His conspicuous absence led to a buildup of things that needed his attention, some immediately, some not so much. At this point the particulars didn't really matter one way or another because his mind wasn't in it. Since the second Unique came clean about everything—old boyfriends and associates, the stint in prison, the cons, being forced to sell her body in Mexico—it was strange that he wasn't really angry with Unique. In fact, the only thing Kennard had on his mind was the sucker called Fat Tee. This fool had the nerve to break into *his* house and rape *his* woman, on *his* kitchen floor. Who in their right mind would think that would even fly?

The lyrics from Jay-Z's "Niggas in Paris" broke his train of thought. His eyes jerked to the iPhone laying dormant on the desk to his right before remembering that he'd powered off the thing. Way past being tired of the constant flood of calls he'd been receiving, mostly from people being nosy or wanting something, with their insincere condolences as a preamble to what they were really after, Kennard realized that the ringing phone was in his pocket, another iPhone. Identical to the one on his desk that he used for business, but this one an untraceable cell phone. It wasn't registered in anyone's name. And only a handful of people had the number. He dug the phone from his pocket, checked the number on the display screen, satisfied of who the caller was, and pushed RECEIVE.

"What up, Drop?" The two were close friends since elementary school—Kennard and Drop-Top went back like the plastic G.I. Joe action figure, before the kung-fu grip.

Drop-Top answered with his usual mantra. "Nothing up but the sun, moon, stars, and modern-day slavery. But that's not why I called."

"Then kill the astronomy lesson and tell me why you called," Kennard said, trying to get to the point.

"I called to put you up on some G. But if you too

busy to parlay . . ." His voice dragged off as if to say he could call back at another time.

Kennard knew Drop-Top like fat chicks swore by Weight Watchers, but yet knew the amount of calories in their favorite Krispy Kreme doughnut.

Drop-Top was a certified, bona fide bad-ass, but even bad-asses wanted to be appreciated.

With a little more enthusiasm in his voice, Kennard asked, "What you got?"

"I was talking to this Brooklyn kid," Drop-Top began. "Dude says he ran into this cat from Virginia trying to off some ice."

Although he was often heavier on the small talk than Kennard would have liked, Drop-Top was like tar and kept his ears pinned to streets and, more often than not, was pinpoint accurate with his information.

"You think it's my boy?" He had Kennard's attention.

The word had been put in the street that Kennard was searching for an out-of-town chump from Virginia called Fat Tee, possibly trying to dump some hot diamonds. Also, it was made clear that anyone who came up with the information leading him to the dude would be well compensated.

Drop-Top said, "That's why I called."

Kennard got up from his seat, made his way to the window overlooking the front lawn. Rain still came down in buckets. "Who's this cat from Brooklyn that dropped the info? And is he reliable?"

"Yeah," Drop-Top said, "I know 'im." It didn't matter which of the five boroughs, if they were in the game, better than average chance that Drop-Top either knew them or knew *of* them. "His name's Bone." The name meant nothing to Kennard. "For the most part a stand-up brotha that fancies himself as a seasoned stick-up kid and a head buster. Said he heard from a friend that a bird from out-of-town was having time, scrambling like two scrambled eggs trying drop some ice. So Bone decided to take the ice and the burden off dude's hands. Said he planned to leave Fat Tee duck-taped and asleep but shit went off plan. Anyway," Drop-Top continued, "I wouldn't even have brought it to you if I didn't think it was one hundred."

For a few seconds, the phone line was monastery-quiet, the only sounds coming from the raindrops that continued to tap its beat on the window as Kennard digested the information Drop-Top had just shared but most of all he wasn't believing his luck.

"So where is he?" Kennard said, breaking the momentary silence.

Drop-Top, unsure if Kennard was referring to Fat Tee or Bone, asked, "Which one?"

"Who do you think?" Kennard quickly answered. "The dead one."

There was no need for any more clarification or direction. Drop-Top hadn't received his moniker because of his penchant for driving convertible whips; the name Drop-Top was *earned*—at age sixteen—from his more than enthusiastic willingness to peel a nigga's fitted cap back. "Say no more." Kennard heard the conviction in his voice when Drop-Top said, "I got it from here. You know you can count on me, bro."

"Roger that."

THE TOOLS OF THE CRAFT

The cold rain continued to fall at a steady pace. A dark, gray morning filled with infinite opportunities but few promises. *Just another typical shitty day in the big city of dreams*, Drop-Top thought as his black Range Rover exited the Brooklyn-Battery Tunnel to the Brooklyn Queens Expressway with Jay-Z and Notorious B.I.G.'s *The Commission* banging from its built-in MP3 player. The fact that B.I.G. and Jay were both Brooklyn natives was purely coincidence. Drop-Top was a fan of both the rappers' flow.

Concealed inside a tricked-out stash box built behind the Rover's dash were three handguns: a Smith & Wesson 9mm, a Glock .40, and his favorite, the .44 Desert Eagle. He was both comfortable and competent with any of, what he called, "the tools of the craft." Tools that he'd learned to respect.

According to Bone, immediately after the *situation* that took place with him and Fat Tee—as if his trying to rob and kill the dude was just some type of misunderstanding—that Fat Tee acted like his shoes were on fire and packed his shit and beat his feet up out of Madelyn's.

This alone made Drop-Top a step behind the prey.

Then Bone told him, "But not to worry"—as always, for precautionary measures, he'd had one of his boys with an eye on the building before and after the sting. The lookout had followed Fat Tee to an off-brand hotel a block off of Atlantic Avenue in Crown Heights.

Drop-Top pulled into the parking deck of the same hotel.

After finding a suitable parking space he turned on the hazard lights. Pushed the cigarette lighter in. Then, with his right foot, he tapped the brake pedal, twice. He heard the mechanical hum from the hydraulic system as the previously concealed compartment behind the dashboard opened, revealing its hardware. Of the three handguns inside, Drop-Top chose the 16-shot blue-steel Smith & Wesson. For three reasons: it was lightweight, easy to handle, and fitted with a machine-threaded silencer. The nine was as quiet as a bashful lover whenever he decided to bust off.

Less than ten minutes later, two crisp big-face Ben Franklins and a smile for the chick at the desk got Drop-Top the room number he was in search of and two more big-faces bought him the keycards for the doors.

Gotta love Brooklyn. Four hundred dollars is about to bring me forty thousand cash from Kennard and this don't even add in what I get from this nigga in the process. He reminded himself that he knew better than to count his eggs before they hatched. But how couldn't he? This was going to be like taking candy from a baby.

According to Shorty Girl working the front desk, the man matching Fat Tee's description copped a couple of rooms on the eleventh floor—1116 and 1118. Drop-Top used the stairs. There was no need involving any more potential witnesses than necessary. Besides, these days most hotel elevators had digital eyes in the ceiling monitoring who came and went.

The cement block stairwell was hot and narrow— absent the smell of urine. It reminded Drop-Top of the ones in the project tenement where he grew up in the Fort Greene projects. His thoughts momentarily drifted back to when he was twelve years old, the first time Kennard had ever come to his house to visit.

Drop-Top—well, everyone still called him Tyrek back then—and Kennard were in his bedroom playing Galaxy on Tyrek's new Saga Genesis when they heard a loud thump, then a crashing sound. They both jumped up to investigate the noise. Both were surprised when they saw Tyrek's mother, Betty, lying on the small kitchen floor, holding her face.

Her boyfriend was standing over top of her. "Why

the fuck you ain't fix me nothing to eat?" His words were slurred. "I bet the hard-head-ass little knuckle-head motherfucker of yours done had something to eat. Haven't he?" Betty was a small, petite woman. Compared to her boyfriend's six-foot frame she appeared childlike herself.

Back then, another year or two before Tyrek would hit his growth spurt, on a good day, he stood only at five feet. Kennard had already passed him in height by at least five inches but none of that even mattered. Without a second thought Tyrek picked up a plate from the sink and slammed it against his mother's boyfriend's head. It caught him solid, breaking right across his dome. But Betty's boyfriend shook off the blow and backhanded Tyrek, so hard that Tyrek slid across until the wall stopped his momentum.

That's when without hesitation Kennard intervened.

His hands were so fast it was hard to keep up with what they were doing. A flurry of quick, short punches to the dude's kidneys bent him over to size.

Kennard's father, a professional boxing trainer, had taught Kennard the craft young. Early on he could tell that his son had the natural-born talent to be a champion one day. Power, speed, and smarts—Kennard had it all. And Kennard unleashed it all on Betty's drunk, abusive boyfriend. A twelve-year-old kid pummeling a grown man into submission; it was a sight to see. It was a display of boxing artistry worthy of a Pay-Per-View slot.

Kennard and Tyrek, being in the same class, were already mad cool, but from that day forward they became brothers.

Three years later, a kid from uptown snatched Kennard's mother's pocketbook. Tyrek got word of who'd done it and with an old Maxima and a .380, Tyrek returned the favor. He caught the dude in front of a trap spot, slipping. The poor purse snatcher had no idea that a kid he'd never met was about to introduce himself. Tyrek said "hello" by way of two quick shots from the automatic handgun, flipping the pocketbook thief's head back and earning the name Drop-Top at the same time.

Kennard's enemy was his enemy. If Kennard hurt, so did Drop-Top. Whoever Kennard liked, Drop-Top had affection for, and this included Unique. She was not only Kennard's woman, she was considered Drop-Top's sister, and nobody violated anybody he cared about.

When Drop-Top reached a metal door with the number 11 stenciled with red paint on the front, his focus returned to the moment. Hinges screamed out like they hadn't seen a drop of lubricant in a century as the door opened.

The hallway was empty.

Around twelve, maybe thirteen rooms were on each side.

The dull brass plate on the first wooden door to his right read *1102*; across the hall, catty-corner to refrain nosy guest from peeping in their neighbor's rooms when the doors were open, was *1101*.

Stoically, not too slow or too fast, Drop continued down the hallway as if he belonged there and owned the place.

1104 . . .

1106 . . .

1108 . . .

1110 . . .

1112 . . .

1114 . . .

At *1116,* he stopped.

Fat Tee was either in this room or the one next door. Drop-Top sighed. It was fifty-fifty. A pistol gripped in his right palm, a keycard in his left, Drop-Top put his ear to the door. He didn't hear anything that would change the odds as they stood. Not even a television going. *Damn.* He shook his head.

Slowly, he slid the keycard into the slot, knowing he could easily be walking into a trap, but willing to risk it. The light on the lock changed from red to green.

Hoping that the door's hinges wasn't as dry as the ones on the stairwell, he pushed open the door to room 1116.

"Maintenance," he said out loud, at that moment hoping that his Dickie's khakis could pass him off as such.

Inside was an average-sized hotel room with a bed, a nightstand, a dresser, a closet, and a bathroom, everything that was supposed to be there . . . but no signs of Fat Tee. The bed looked as if it hadn't even been slept in. With his pistol leading the way, Drop-Top checked the bathroom just to be sure. Satisfied that the room was empty, he walked out as quietly as he'd entered.

1118.

Ear to the door; he didn't hear any sounds coming from this one, either. He was hopeful that he'd caught the dude asleep. Drop-Top slipped the card into the lock the same as he'd done next door, making virtually no noise.

With the silencer of the nine taking the lead, he stepped in, primed and ready.

Fat Tee was lying underneath the cover. Apparently the dude was a late sleeper. *Where you're going,* Drop-top thought, *you'll be able to sleep as long as you want.*

Index finger caressing the trigger, Drop-Top squeezed. Twice.

Phssst! Phssst!

The pair of hollow-points barely made a sound as they flew from the barrel of the nine, slamming into the body of Fat Tee.

To be sure that the job was complete and Fat Tee wasn't still sucking in oxygen, Drop-Top walked up to the bed with a smile cut across his face and pulled back the covers. What should've been a corpse were three fucking pillows.

A handwritten note was laying on the one where the head should've been, a bullet hole in its center.

Fuck you! Try again! You bitch-ass New York niggas . . .

"Those VA cats weren't as dumb as they looked," Drop-Top said to himself as he left the room. "But we'll see who gets the last laugh, VA—we'll see!"

KARMA IS A MOTHER . . .

Since the big confession, Kennard hadn't said much to Unique, who had been tiptoeing around the house, trying to give him space to figure out what he wanted to do with their relationship. The energy in their home had been off since she had poured out her heart to him about her past. Even on the chilliest New York night, it had never been that cold between the two of them.

She couldn't really blame him and took it as if he was just trying to digest everything that she had told him the night before. She didn't like it but what could she do? She was grateful that he hadn't asked her to leave yet. In fact, she was thinking about going to stay at her friend Tyeedah's house until his head was clear.

This wasn't the way she had planned it, but she was willing to accept the consequences of her actions.

She was in the den, watching Lifetime, preparing herself because she was certain that her life was about to play out like a movie. She could hear him on the phone, and she had decided that when the flick was over she was to get up and get dinner going. Though she knew he was talking to someone, she couldn't make out the words because she wasn't ear hustling—she didn't want to get in his way by any means.

As she watched the last scene of the movie, tears started to form in her eyes and that's when Kennard poked his head in the room. "Yo, throw on your sweats and sneakers and come on."

She perked up quickly. "Where we going?" She was glad to go anywhere with him—or glad he wanted her to go somewhere with him.

"We're going to deal with that nigga, Fat Tee's bitch ass," he said in a nonchalant way, but she knew it was about to get serious.

Kennard had put the word out on the street looking for Fat Tee and had gotten an inside tip from a desk clerk that he was laying low at a hotel in the Bronx.

"Awww, baby." She was so happy that Kennard still cared. Unique could not believe that Kennard was going to roll out for her like this. This made her love him more and though she, more than anybody, wanted Fat Tee to get what he had coming to him, she didn't want Kennard to get in any kind of trouble. "Thank you so much but I don't want you to get caught up in this bullshit."

"When that nigga had the balls to enter *my* house and rape not just any woman but *my* woman, then had the gall to put his hands on you, that mother-fucker made his own death wish."

"But he ain't worth you getting involved."

"Baby, him making you lose my baby . . . Look, I understand that you have been through enough with this nigga so if you wanna stay here while I go deal with this problem, then I understand. But it might be the best therapy for you to see firsthand this mother-fucker get his and hear him beg you for his shitty-ass, worthless, two-bit life!" Kennard emphasized every word he said but he wanted to see them wheel Fat Tee's lifeless body out of the hotel under the white sheet.

"Oh no, baby! If you go, baby, I go!"

Unique tied her sneakers up and was on the way out of the door when the TV bolted to the wall caught her attention. She had turned to the evening news. They were broadcasting a story about stolen diamonds. The story stopped Unique in her tracks and led her to pick up the remote from the table beside the bed and turn up the sound.

"Babe, babe," Unique screamed out for Kennard at the top of his lungs, "come quick."

Kennard came rushing into the bedroom. "What's wrong, babe?" He heard the volume of the television up loud and saw the stunned look on her face that was focused on the tube, which prompted him to immediately give his attention to the news' breaking story as well.

They both stood and listened to the newscaster's report.

"Thirty-one-year-old Mr. Terrell Gump, from Richmond, Virginia, was apprehended by TSA at LaGuardia Airport yesterday after a body scanner revealed that he had an unusual-shaped mass lodged in his anus." She seemed to be fighting the urge to laugh as she read the teleprompter. "After a perfunctory cavity search," she continued, besting her emotions, "the object turned out to be an estimated 1.2 million dollars' worth of stolen diamonds."

The producers cut to a still frame of the hot ice lying on a table. The shiny gems glistened under the camera's light.

With a WTF expression on her face, Unique looked on with Kennard. The temperature of her blood going from warm to white hot, both nervous and shocked, her mouth opened, forming the shape of doughnut.

The screen switched back to the anchor, Pamela Pitchford.

"Sergeant McDaniel of the NYPD said that Mr. Gump had allegedly been trying to sell the stolen diamonds—one at a time—to various underground jewelers. The problem, which Mr. Gump obviously wasn't aware, was that the diamonds were registered, making each diamond identifiable. There was also a tracking device in the bag in which they were originally stolen, which for some reason Mr. Gump kept."

They showed a mug shot of the suspect: a dark-skin dude with a mouth full of silver teeth.

The two worst-looking pictures in the world always seemed to be DMV's and a mug shot and his mug shot didn't do Fat Tee one bit of justice.

"If convicted, Mr. Gump could get up to life in prison," Pamela Pitchford pointed out.

Her co-anchor chimed in: "That's a long time to serve for trying to dodge a luggage fee. . . . In other news . . ."

"Yo, that shit is crazy."

"It is!"

"Better that the spooks get him than me, I guess," Kennard said, disappointed, but there was still a devilish grin plastered all over his face.

Unique was kind of relieved because she really didn't want Kennard getting his hands dirty on that trash Fat Tee.

But Kennard now had a puzzled look on his face.

"What's wrong?" Unique asked.

"I just hope this bitch-ass nigga don't start talking when he gets to the pen, that's all."

Unique knew that what he was saying was true and was most likely going to happen. Fat Tee hated her guts and there was no reason he wouldn't tell on her. It's not like he even lived by the morals and principles of the streets. That's why they were in the situation to start with: Fat Tee didn't pay Took when Took went to jail because he had no regard for the rules of the dope game, which then caused Took to want revenge and his money. This then prompted Took to go to extreme measures to get what he felt like he was owed and to make a point that nobody does that kind of shit to him.

Fat Tee indeed got a huge dose of his own medicine and then Unique not only played a big part in hitting him where it hurt—his pockets—but she hurt his feelings and made him the laughingstock of the hood.

All these things confirmed any thoughts that Unique had, and tears formed in her eyes. "I'm pretty sure that Fat Tee is going to tell on me. As soon as he gets there he's going to start singing like a songbird in a chorus line. That you can bet."

"Don't worry your pretty face, I will take care of it."

"Easier said than done."

"Trust me!"

And she did . . . that's all she could do. She had learned the hard way what could happen when she took things into her own hands.

RIKERS

Someone great once said, "The ultimate measure of man is not where he stands in moments of comfort and convenience, but where he stands at times of challenge and controversy."

Fat Tee had no idea why that damn quote kept popping into his head.

Sitting at one of the metal tables in the dayroom, Fat Tee kept trying to remember where he had heard it before. He thought it had been MLK, Jr. He wanted to quote it in the letter to his attorney. He decided to move on to his next letter, and tried to focus on blocking everything out. He wanted to take his time to pen this letter, to be sure and give the details to his partner back home in Virginia of everything that had transpired with Unique and the diamonds. Though he might have to do a little time, best believe her ass was going to pay in more ways than one. The latter made him smile to himself. She was going to get hers.

The noise was so loud that he couldn't concentrate.

Dudes in his pod were playing cards, watching the game, talking on the phone, and plotting against each other—he could barely hear himself think. If his cellie hadn't asked for "private time," Fat Tee could have written his letters in there—he would at least have been able to hear himself think.

Fat Tee had been in the infamous Rikers Island jail for seven days now, and in that time he'd been in two fights and gotten his butt kicked both times but at least he fought back. He knew he wasn't going to be able to do his bid like this. Rikers was tough enough as it was, but not being from New York put him at a major disadvantage—a foreigner in a foreign land didn't usually fare well in prison. Shit, he might as well have gotten arrested in Mexico or Thailand.

He touched the flattened piece of cold steel that was concealed under his shirt between the waistband of his pants and his side to make sure it was still there. He'd bought the knife off a Puerto Rican for fifty dollars, which he sold his sneakers to get. The knife gave him some comfort, but not much. The new kid always had to prove that he wasn't a chump before someone else proved that he was. That was the way the machine worked. And Fat Tee knew, in his heart, he wasn't built for this shit.

He was counting down the days until Friday, when Fat Tee's lawyer had promised to get him a face-to-face with the DA. If Fat Tee gave up the people he claimed he'd gotten the diamonds from, and it all panned out, they could make a deal.

Fat Tee had absolutely no problem giving up Unique's ass. Better her than him. The only thing he was upset about was that he didn't know the name of that tight-ass bitch that was with her. But in the end it didn't matter. He had no intention of taking the rap. FUCK THAT!

Fat Tee dropped the letter in the mail to his partner and then went back to his cell to get the address for his lawyer. Cats were giving him the screw face. Nothing new. *These up-north niggas thought that they were all that,* he thought, *that's why we send them back in body bags when they tried to hustle in Richmond.*

He hoped his cellie was finish beating his dick, or whatever it was he needed to be alone for. Their cell was on the upper floor. To get up the steps he had to walk through a maze of mean-mugging convicts.

"Pardon me," he said, sliding through the gauntlet of thugs to get to the second floor. Never missing the opportunity to show that they had the upper hand on him, they acted like they didn't want to move out of his way. They paid him as much attention as they would an annoying fly. The tension was thick as day-old oatmeal.

Making it to the top of the stairs without incident was a chore in itself. Fat Tee quickly walked to his cell and saw that his cellie was gone. Good, he thought. Maybe he could get a few minutes of "private time" for himself.

Inside the cell, and lying on the bottom bunk, was a *Straight Stuntin* magazine and a bottle of lotion. Fat Tee started to close the metal door to the cell when it stopped cold on its steel hinges. A boot had stopped it from closing.

Then the owner of the boot, along with a friend, pushed his way in, and shut the door behind them.

Fat Tee said, "My cellie ain't here," not knowing what else to say.

One of the dudes that had bombarded their way into his cell sported a bald head, was six-foot-four or better, and built like the Incredible Hulk. His side-kick was his polar opposite. He was barely over five-foot-five and seemed childlike.

"We ain't checking for your cellie, bee," the Incredible Hulk said, flexing his muscles. "We here to deliver a message to you."

The cell was small—six by nine—and with three people standing inside, they were already crowding each other's space.

Fat Tee tried to relax. The fingers of his right hand were twitching as they hovered near his waist, inches away from the knife. He hoped that he wouldn't need it, but if he did he was ready.

Looking the Hulk straight in the eyes, Fat Tee asked, "Who is the message from, man?"

Hulk smiled like he'd just won the lottery and taken the one lump sum before saying with great pride, "Kennard."

It took a beat for the name to register, and another heartbeat before it meant anything to him. Kennard, the man whose fiancée he'd raped, blackmailed, disrespected, assaulted, and nearly killed. A frigid fear, cold as the steel under his shirt, flowed through his veins.

Hulk said, "He wanted to send his regards . . . and his condolences." The sound in Hulk's voice had the finality of the lid closing on a casket.

Fat Tee swallowed the lump in his throat and his fear in one gulp. Both went down hard. The line had been drawn. He knew that this altercation would only resolve itself with bloodshed. Fat Tee reached for his knife, his eyes never swaying from the dead irises of Hulk.

Fat Tee had his blade—a six-inch piece of flattened steel—firmly in his hand before the Incredible Hulk even knew what happened. This wasn't his first fucking barbecue. Fat Tee knew what it felt like to kill a man, and had no problem experiencing that feeling again, déjà-fucking-vu. His only regret was that he hadn't set it off on one of these fools off the break.

Fat Tee watched the Hulk's eyes as they tracked the movement of the knife arcing toward his head. Hulk tensed, causing a vein to bulge in the side of his neck. Fat Tee beamed in on the vein, using it as his target. He saw fear bungee-jump into Hulk's eyes.

They were grossly mistaken if they thought he would lie down and be punked simply because he was outnumbered. Niggas from the R didn't roll like that, he thought, as the knife in his hand got closer to sending its own message. Fuck Kennard and the Hulk.

The blade found its target and went in smooth and easy.

Shock replaced the fear in Hulk's eyes.

But it wasn't the shock of being stabbed in his jugular or the shock of bleeding to death in a jail cell. It was the shock of being taken out by an out-of-towner.

Fat Tee had underestimated Hulk's little sidekick, who was actually the real threat.

Though Junior was twenty-two years old, he looked to be no older than fifteen years old, and nobody on God's green earth would judge from looking at him that he was a certified stone-cold killer. And when Kennard found out that BG was on the island, he sent word for him to do what he did best. And though it was greatly appreciated when Kennard dropped 10Gs off at his momma's house, Junior would have killed Fat

Tee for a box of cupcakes. The truth of the matter was that he got off on it.

Junior's ice pick penetrated Fat Tee's side like a Ginsu knife going though warm butter. With the speed of a Chinese prep cook, Junior brought the blade end out, six or seven times, at the blink of an eye, crippling Fat Tee.

Fat Tee tried to grab the pointed steel skewer sticking out from his kidneys like some type of sick human shish kebab, when he got hit again in the neck. Hulk had backed away to the door. *How many hands did the lil dude have?* Fat Tee thought as he started to lose consciousness.

Fat Tee reached for the ice pick protruding from his neck.

Fat Tee could feel the life dripping out of his body as the hired killers kept jack-hammering away with the two ice picks. He felt his body weakening. He was losing too much blood to survive, but that was the idea, right?

Junior had finally stopped stabbing him. No need for the overkill, like he'd done Unique. They left him in the dark room alone.

Fat Tee fought to stay alive but all he could hear in his head was his grandma's voice, saying the same thing over and over like a scratched record: "Boy, if you don't start believing in karma, you might as well go ahead and be an atheist and not believe in God. Because what you do to others will be done to you!"

In that cold jail cell, alone, far away from home, Fat Tee fought to stay alive.

But like premature ejaculation, death came quick.

EPILOGUE
BACK IN VIRGINIA

Always something interesting in the Metro section of the newspaper, thought Took as he tossed the morning paper on the kitchen table, smirking at the fact that he *did* know who the murdered "unidentified men" were who were plastered over the front page of the *Richmond Times Dispatch.* And he also knew that they deserved exactly what they got. Loose lips sank ships and theirs had gone down like the *Titanic.*

He looked at his watch: 1:00 P.M. *Damn the day is moving fast,* he thought.

He needed to be across town by two and wanted to stop and get something to eat on the way. After locking up his place, he made his way down the three flights of concrete stairs—two at a time—and once reaching the bottom, he stopped at the lobby's recessed mailboxes. He wasn't expecting anything, but the mailman had been leaving him threatening notes on his door for not cleaning out all the junk mail. In return, Took had left the mailman a note that said

"Stop leaving that shit." But at the end of the day Took knew he did too much dirt to draw unnecessary attention to himself. So he decided this was the day he'd retrieve the mail.

Took's box was marked: APT. 306.

Besides the junk mail, to Took's surprise, there was one letter addressed to him and the most surprising part was that the letter was postmarked from New York.

The return address read:

Rikers Island Jail
Terrell Gump #1143667
18-18 Hazen St.
East Elmhurst, New York   11370

For a minute Took didn't recall the name, then, suddenly, it hit him. Terrell Gump was Fat Tee. *But what THE FUCK was Fat Tee doing locked up in New York? And more important, why the fuck is this motherfucker writing me?*

They weren't cool. In fact, Fat Tee and Took had shared more bad blood than good. And if Fat Tee thought that Took would come to his rescue by making his bond, Fat Tee better have had a plan B, because he was S-O-L (shit out of luck) on plan A. On general principle Took wasn't even going to open the envelope. Then he quickly changed his mind. *Shit, let me see what the fuck dis nigga talking 'bout.* It wouldn't cost him anything but a few seconds of his time to read the damn thing anyways. Maybe even get a good laugh out of it. Then throw it away.

The letter began:

Took:
I know getting a fucking letter from me was the last thing you were expecting. I've been thinking about this shit long and hard for the past week, and you were the one person that I knew that had as big of an ax to grind with Unique as I did . . .

The mention of Unique's name caught Took off guard, like an unexpected left hook to the dome. Unique was the first chick he ever made the mistake of trusting. She was supposed to be his "ride or die" but when Took got knocked she jumped ship. The no-good, two-bit broad jacked off the eighty grand he'd left in her care, and didn't even have the decency to take his calls or put one iron dime on his books for that matter.

He'd be lying if he said that he never thought about her. Sometimes, the thoughts were even good ones, but usually, not so much. He was anxious to hear what the latest news on her was; the last time he'd seen or heard anything from Unique, he'd sold her to Jose in Mexico for two chickens, a mule and a key of co-caine. The chickens, because she was a chickenhead.

The mule, because she'd made a jackass out of him and the key of cocaine was just a bonus.

That bitch is living the life of luxury with a nigga name Kennard DuVall, real made nigga—Google that nigga— and see the empire this motherfucker sitting on. I'ma fix this bitch, decided I'm going to let the state of New York deal with the bitch—but him . . . I will give you on a silver platter. And I'm in hopes that you will just break me off, but some of that cheddar by way of putting my finder's fee on my books.

MOB—all day my nigga! Let bygones be bygones and get that nigga however or for whatever you can.

PS: I know for a fact that Unique has persuaded this nigga to get revenge on you for leaving her in Mexico. Get that nigga before he gets you!

UNIQUE III: REVENGE

THE EPITOME OF BALLING

The party, hands down, was the hottest ticket in the city tonight.

So hot that an underground bootlegger inked fifty additional invites, identical to the real thing, and put them up on the Internet and made them available to the highest bidders, who were not privileged enough to get on the guest list. The knock-offs started at $2,500 a pop . . . and were gone less than an hour after hitting the black market. Took wasn't going to miss this for anything in the world. He was determined to get to the party and it was nothing but God's grace and mercy that he managed to stumble upon one of the fakes. The bogus invite set him back five Gs. Then he forked out another G for the black-and-white mandatory monkey suit and another $800 for the Ferragamo shoes to match his tux. He didn't complain one bit; it was the best seven thousand dollars he'd spent in a real long time. But this was one shindig he wasn't going to miss.

Took stood in the corner and took it all in. Roulette,

slot machines, blackjack, and crap tables transformed the Icon Club into a swanky high-roller casino. Reveling among the timeless games of chance—rubbing elbows and $1,000 chips—were a combination of entrepreneurs, athletes, entertainers, and hustlers donned in tailored tuxedos at the black-tie affair. The gorgeous honeys, in full hunt mode, armed with big smiles and even bigger butts and short dresses, outnumbered their counterparts by at least two-to-one.

Took smiled and nodded in approval. As much as he might've wanted to, he couldn't deny or hate for one second that the hostess of this elaborate celebration had definitely done an opulently fantastic job of laying out the platinum carpet for the guest of honor, who happened to be her newly married husband and renowned boxing promoter Kennard DuVall.

Took didn't know the man from Adam, but he wasn't hard to spot. He took another sip of his drink and checked out the birthday boy from head to toe as DuVall made his way around the room greeting his guests. Tonight was definitely his night and Took had to give it up because the dude didn't half step. The invitation had said to come formally dressed to impress and the invitees followed the directions well. However, DuVall was definitely suited and booted in a way that nobody could steal his shine.

Took had to give credit where credit was due: Kennard was clean as hell in his custom-made purple velvet tuxedo. It could have turned out like Prince in *Purple Rain,* but Kennard pulled it off, with a bow tie, and cummerbund to match. He nailed the ensemble together with some custom gator-and-ostrich-skinned shoes with different shades of purple that blended perfectly.

Took had done his research after receiving the letter about Unique from his source, Fat Tee, and for once, he found that the no-good cocksucker wasn't exaggerating. In fact, Took had come across a *Forbes* magazine piece that estimated Kennard's earnings for the last year at $150 million. Whether in the streets or while doing a media interview, whenever Kennard was asked if *Forbes*'s numbers were correct, his answer was always the same: "It doesn't matter. Regardless of what a person earns, if he spends more than he makes he's guaranteed to go broke."

Then he would grace them with his trademark smile. And whoever had asked the nosy-ass question in the first place would smile along with him.

Really? What did they think he would say?

Hell, Kennard was born a product of Harlem U.S.A., raised in the streets among the rest of the rats. And in the streets, Took had been taught that a man who went around spouting off about what type of chips he stacked was nothing more than a clown that wanted people to believe that he was something he wasn't. But Took wasn't mad. He gave the interviewer the old brush-off; he knew that when a true hustler stacked more cake than anyone could even imagine, he kept it to himself. That's what made Took get his shit right and make his way to the big city to get up close and personal, to see if it was all fluff and talk. And Took observed that Kennard was definitely the real deal holyfield.

It was DuVall's thirty-sixth birthday and Took was surprised that Kennard's new wife, Unique, had every single detail in place. Between the many ice sculptures, the beautiful flowers all strategically placed around the room, the models strutting around in body paint, and the drinks constantly flowing, she had done it up for her husband. And since she was now a chef and had recently opened up her own restaurant, one that Kennard had given her for a wedding present, she didn't cut corners when it came to the food. Before he left, Took intended on trying out every one of the gourmet food stations prepared by chefs from all around the world, which were set up throughout the club. Damn right he was going to get every dollar's worth that he had invested in this trip.

As he stood off near the huge ice sculpture and surveyed the room, he locked eyes with a big, light-skinned guy that looked kind of familiar to him. The world was small, but Took knew that none of the folks he rolled with, ran in the same circles as Kennard. So, he quickly dismissed him as one of Kennard's celebrity friends' security detail.

After someone whispered something in the big guy's ear and he walked off into the crowd, dude became an afterthought. Took accepted another drink off of the tray of the waitress passing by. He thought about what he had invested, it was a small amount of money to get exactly what he wanted. There was only one problem: he still wasn't sure exactly what he wanted from Unique.

The relationship Took and Unique had shared in the past, so many years ago, had been . . . eventful.

In the beginning, they had been like Bonnie and Clyde—ride or die, living out life like the Tupac song, he and she against the world. Back then, the Unique he knew was as shiesty as she was beautiful, two lethal characteristics that had attracted him to her. Took often wondered if they would've still been together if she hadn't quit taking his calls after he got pinched by the police and sent to prison. She had blown through every single penny of the eighty Gs he had left with her. At that time it was all the paper Took had to his name, and the most fucked-up part of it was that he could have left it with his mother or grandmother for safe-keeping, but he didn't think twice about trusting his girl. *When the money was gone . . . Unique was gone,* was the chant with which his cellies would tease him.

After Unique stopped taking his calls, all he had left was time.

Time to plan.

This was one instance when time didn't heal his wounds, heart, or ego.

"May I help you with a drink, hon?"

The chick with the long sexy eyelashes and a tray of crystal flutes filled with yellow-colored bubbly got his attention. Took looked her over from head to toe—the woman looked too good to be serving drinks. But he was familiar with her kind. It was clear she was simply playing her position as a barmaid until a better one presented itself, one that she could take advantage of.

"Sure." Took gloved one of the flutes from the tray, and offered the server a smile, looked her over again, and said, "Thanks," before taking a sip of the bubbly. The provocative sway of the server's hips as she sashayed off was her way of saying, "You're welcome."

Took watched from across the room as his ex-girlfriend Unique engaged with her guests. She was dressed in a long, elegant, form-fitting, purple backless gown made out of the same material as Kennard's tux. She had definitely evolved, but still had her same walk though she had grown into a more beautiful woman.

His feelings for Unique were bittersweet. In one

way, he despised her for always being able to survive, with or without his help. In another way, one that he'd never admit to anyone, he was proud of her, of what she'd become and how she had taken a busted hand and turned it into a straight flush. That was one of the things he had always loved about her—she knew how to take nothing and turn it into something. She knew how to play the game and knew the right buttons to push with any man. To feed his own ego, he took credit for Unique being the beautiful, freaky, charismatic, could-hook-a-steak-up, good-pussy-having, bad bitch that she was today and had always been. *Damn, I always knew how to pick 'em,* he thought, wanting to give himself a pat on the back.

The promotional campaign that the makers of Virginia Slims cigarettes used to push their cancer sticks was, "You've come a long way, baby." This certainly fit the little bull-headed, cat-eyed girl that just happened to be born and bred in the city of Richmond, Virginia.

Took was still in awe of how everything had turned out for Unique. He reflected on the letters he had written her many years ago from jail and about the rumors he would hear about her messing with two-bit hustlers, who didn't measure up to half of who he was, to get what she needed to get by after she had run through his money. He recollected how he would tell her, "If you're going to leave me, make sure you take a step up with somebody above my level, but never a step down." And all these years he thought his words had been falling on deaf ears. This proved that she must have been listening . . . as much as he didn't want to admit, Kennard was definitely a step up.

Kennard was only a few feet away from him and Took decided to move in closer to ear hustle a little more.

Kennard walked over to a guy, the size of a tank, standing over one of the three crap tables, tossing ivory bones.

The Tank shouted, "Nina Ross!" in search of a nine on the dice, as he scooted the bones down the length of the red felt–lined gaming table. The bones, either not hearing him or not taking requests, stopped on seven.

When the houseman barked out, "Loser!" the Tank cringed.

"Next shooter," said the houseman.

Before the Tank could place another bet, Kennard tapped him on the shoulder. The Tank spun around with the grace of a dancer. The ease with which he moved seemed odd for a man of his size.

Kennard—no small dude himself—stood at least four inches shorter and was considerably lighter in mass and muscle.

"Let me rap with you for a second," he said with a

swag that made it clear who the real "Big Man" in the room was . . . . And it wasn't the Tank.

That's when Took noticed for the first time that the Tank was actually former heavyweight boxing champion of the world, Billy "Grimm-Reaper" Jones. Boxers had literally fought for their lives when they got into the square with him.

Apparently not in the mood for talking, Grimm-Reaper asked, "Can it wait? I'm behind right now," which was the story of his life.

It was widely known that Billy Jones gambled compulsively—just one of the many bad habits he possessed.

Shaking his head, Kennard said, "No Grimm, it can't wait." Then he paused and asked, "Unless you want to throw away a chance of a lifetime, for the second time in your life?"

Kennard had invested a lot of bread in resurrecting the ex-champion's career, and didn't intend to allow his investment to fall by the wayside.

"So, you got everything ironed out with the purse. Man, Kennard, my money is still fucked up, in the worst way. I'm going to need an advance on that purse."

"You already pawned off half of your purse, man. However I'm going to see if I can get you a few dollars to hold you over. In the meantime, you need to fall back from the tables, booze and women," Kennard firmly said. "But most importantly you need to get your ass back to camp first thing Monday morning."

"Yes, I will. On the first thing smoking after I swing by your office to get that check and get it to the bank. Matter of fact, I hate to ask you on your birthday— but you got a couple of stacks on you I can hold until I get that loot from you on Monday?"

Took read Kennard's expression and it said, "Nigga, you got to be outta yo mind, you begging for presents on my birthday." But he kept his composure. After all, it was business. He said, "See me before you leave."

As Kennard finished his lightweight conversation with the heavyweight, he walked off and made his way over to another fella. Took had no idea who he was either, but he soon eased his way over to find out. In the midst of playing his position he couldn't seem to keep his eyes off of Unique who was now having a conversation with another beautiful woman, who looked to be a friend. As soon as the other lady walked off, Unique took a glass off of the waitress tray, sipped a little of the bubbly and started to look over the room, making sure everything was in order.

Took caught himself staring at Unique and when she made eye contact with him, he could see how her entire facial expression and body language changed.

She looked like she was about to either faint or shit a brick. He knew she couldn't believe her eyes, and he smiled at the priceless look on her face. He lifted his glass to her and she sashayed off quickly toward her husband.

Took was entertained and was ready for whatever was about to go down. He was prepared for security to throw him out or for Unique to approach him and make a scene. To keep his composure, he redirected his attention to the two up-and-coming boxers across the room who were verbally sparring, using words as if they were sticks of dynamite, as to which one had dibs on a certain young lady's assets. Thick in all the right places, the brick house they were arguing over seemed more than willing to share her talents with the highest bidder. In a field this loaded with bad bitches, her talents, whatever they were, must be legendary because it seemed like it was about to go down.

"Nigga, she don't want you," Thunderbolt said. "Get that through your skull."

"And she damn sure don't want your herpes-carrying ass," Tee-Quick said.

Thunderbolt, who was wearing a cream-colored double-breasted suit and a dub hat, smiled before he spoke. "Well, if I got herpes, then so do you. 'Cause everything she done did to you, she done did to me and my homeboy a hundred times over. So, we all better go get tested." He took a pull on his cigar.

As Unique made her way across the room, Took moved so she lost sight of him, but he was still close enough to be within earshot of Kennard, so he could hear whatever it was that Unique was going to say to him. *Wonder what she's gonna conjure up to tell this nigga?* Took thought, humoring himself.

As she approached Kennard, Took took another sip of his drink. *This shit right here is about to get good.*

"John, have I introduced you to my beautiful wife, Unique?" Kennard asked the fella he was talking to, while taking her hand.

"Damn." There was a pause as the man checked her out. "I mean, no, you haven't." John's eyes were glued to Unique. Took watched as the guy undressed Unique with his eyeballs, then listened as he tried to stroke Kennard's ego. "You were too busy trying to blow up your already morbidly obese bank account. But I now see why."

"Put your tongue back in your face before I snatch that motherfucker out." Kennard said it jokingly, but was dead serious. Then he turned back to Unique. "Baby, this googly-eyed clown's name is John Bookerman. If I can get him to stop counting my chips and staring at my wife, I think we could get some business done."

Unique smiled at Kennard, but Took knew that

was her way of trying to hide that something was indeed wrong, and it made Took feel good that Kennard couldn't see beyond Unique's poker face. *Maybe they weren't as madly in love as they portrayed to the world,* Took thought to himself.

"Nice to meet you, John. I'm sure you guys will work it all out," she said curtly. "But, do you mind if I steal my husband for a second?"

"Take a couple of minutes if you need to," said John. "That husband of yours could talk an angel out of his only pair of wings. I can use a few minutes to regroup from his tough negotiations." John took a swallow of his drink and walked away. Took rolled his eyes at John who peeped Took ear hustling. *"Get off that nigga dick,"* he said under his breath, but the man kept it moving and tried to catch up with a Miss America chick. It was annoying the hell out of Took that he couldn't recall her name. But he wasn't going to get distracted with John and the beauty queen—he wanted to hear the convo at hand.

"What's going, baby?" Kennard turned and looked into her eyes and Took knew from the way he held her in his arms that DuVall could finally sense that something was really bothering Unique, especially for her to chase the paper away. "Are you okay?"

Before Unique could answer, someone screamed out, *"Fight!"*

Together, Unique and Kennard turned and watched as everyone started gathering near the smoked glass of the VIP suite, to look at the floor below. Unique and Kennard, reflexively, didn't join the crowd. Kennard wasn't overly concerned since he'd hired enough security, bouncers, and off-duty police officers to protect Obama if the brother had wanted to attend. Still, he put his arms around his wife as if he were going to protect her above everything else.

"It's Thunderbolt and Tee-Quick," somebody said.

"I got a thou on Tee-Quick," said another guest.

"Make it five and you got a bet."

"Done."

"I bet they're rumbling over that gold-digging bitch, Pinky," John said, as he walked up to Kennard.

"They couldn't save that shit for the ring?" Kennard shot back as he went for a look.

"Yeah, that bitch been going between the two of them for years now. Dealing with whoever holding the biggest purse. I thought the niggas had accepted that she comes with the belt—whoever wins is who she is with," John joked.

"Unbelievable," Kennard said. Tee-Quick was one of his fighters. While he was trying to make the deal with John for those two fools to go at it in the ring on Pay-Per-View for $40 million, they were brawling it out in the middle of the club, becoming the entertainment for his birthday party. "These some stupid-ass niggas. I can understand the Patrón may have them a little riled up, but over this stinking broad, Pinky?" That pissed Kennard off.

The woman with pink hair and a body like a super-hero looked back and forth, saying, "Fellas, stop it," as she tried to calm them both down, but the look in her eyes said that she was loving every minute of the two prizefighters fighting over her.

Amid all the commotion, Took slipped away . . . like a ghost.

OUT OF GAS

Morning." The sure grin Seymour sported made him look even cuter than he already was. "My apologies for running out of gas on you last night," he said with a smile as he kissed her on his forehead.

Tyeedah's vajayjay was still sore from all the screwing they'd done, but she still wanted him more than a kid wanted candy. She assured him, "You have absolutely nothing at all to be sorry about. I was running on pure fumes last night." A coy smile took over her face as she hopped on top of him and looked into his eyes. "Fumes and good dick," she said to him with a big smile of pleasure.

Her mainframe hadn't been serviced this well since . . . well, much longer than she wanted to remember or admit.

Seymour, hands already under the comforter, gripped her butt, then pinched her on the cheek.

"A brother is only as good as his motivation," he said to her, and then gave her a long tongue kiss.

"You know kissing is intimate, right?" Tyeedah asked, pulling back to lock eyes with him.

"Well, let's get intimate then," he said, giving her an even longer kiss, surprising even himself. He normally never kissed any woman on the mouth. It was a rule he had adopted a long time ago. But for some reason he didn't care about breaking his own law, because in a strange way this felt right.

"I don't become intimate with just any guy," she said with a raised eyebrow when they came up for air.

"Well, let me assure you"—he leaned in as close as he could—"I'm not just any ole dude; I'm unlike any man you will ever meet in your life." He looked in her eyes unblinkingly and said with authority, "I promise you that."

There was something about this guy. The way he looked at her and took control of her body—there was no denying the dude was not only cute and charming, but he also had the swagger of a performer and was a true dick technician. All the things that she knew she needed and wanted in her life. "I thought cats from V-A were supposed to be country, backwoods-types of guys," Tyeedah joked, then batted her eyes and asked, "Where're you really from?"

Seymour laughed. "The country and backwoods?" He smacked his hand against his thigh. "I'm from the capital city of Virginia," he said. "Not West Virginia."

The image of the moonshine-toting redneck try-ing to seduce a sister brought out his own laughter. It was funny how people always seemed to get Virginia and West Virginia mixed up. She laughed with Sey-mour, realizing that she was so comfortable with him. The way they were vibing each other and the things they had done between those sheets, it was hard to believe they had met only two days ago.

Inside of the Icon Club, during Kennard's birthday party, Tyeedah had been on her way back upstairs to the VIP room to look for Unique. No more than fifteen minutes had elapsed since she'd told Unique that she was going to run downstairs to say hello to someone.

That's when she saw him standing near the Mu-hammad Ali ice sculpture, alone. While she was carry-ing on a conversation with a friend of hers, she couldn't stop staring at him. Ruggedly handsome, he was in-deed her type. When she was on her way back to the VIP section, something overtook her. Not sure if it was the rosé wine or just his pull, Tyeedah boldly ap-proached him and said, "Hi, how are you doing? My name is Tyeedah."

He didn't say anything to her at first. She thought perhaps he didn't hear her because of the music, so she repeated herself, a little louder. He still didn't budge or acknowledge her. She thought to herself, *Maybe he's mute, deaf, or just a plain asshole.* Whatever it was, she wasn't going to let his nonresponse crush her ego or blow her high. *Forgive him, Father, this dude don't know what's good for him.*

Just when she was about to walk away, he spoke. "I'm sorry, baby." He smiled at her. "Did you say something to me, gorgeous?" He looked her up and down in a sexy way and said, "Besides, you need to be mine."

"Really?" She wasn't expecting those words and she decided to hear him out.

"That's right," he said in the cockiest way. "Pardon me, beautiful, my mind was somewhere else. I'm Seymour. And you are?"

"I'm Tyeedah." She offered a smile. The chemistry was good right from the start. "You're from down South, huh." It was more of a statement than a question.

He had a bright smile and his tooth, left side, in the front, sported a gold crown. "What gave me away?"

"My best friend is from down South; you both have that same accent."

They'd been talking for about five minutes, when someone yelled, "Thunderbolt is about to whip Tee-Quick's ass!"

As some of the crowd of wealthy partygoers moved toward the action, the two of them looked at each other, smiled, and headed the other way, dipping out the auxiliary exit.

"Where to?" Seymour asked once their feet hit the busy New York street.

Tyeedah, already flagging down a cab, said, "I'm hungry. I was too busy socializing all night and we left before I could eat anything."

"Where you wanna go?" he asked.

Without hesitation, she said, "I know where they sell the best pizza in New York."

"Aren't we a little overdressed for pizza?" Seymour asked as he climbed into the backseat of a yellow cab next to Tyeedah, willing to go somewhere a little more high-end.

"You are in the Big Apple now, baby," she said in her thickest New York accent. "You can never be too sharp to grab a few slices in the city."

After a couple pizzas and beers, they talked for hours. They watched the sun rise over the city from the window of his hotel room. The next day, after a morning filled with hot sex, they went out to get her a change of clothes, followed by lunch in Central Park, a tour of the Statue of Liberty, and a horse-and-carriage ride while watching the sunset. The climax of the day literally happened back at his hotel room again for the rest of the evening and all of the night.

Tyeedah was awakened by Took opening the curtains.

"Good morning, gorgeous," he said when he realized she was up.

"Good morning, baby" she said, immediately reaching for her purse. "How did you sleep?"

The bright sunlight was bringing Tyeedah back to reality. As beautiful as the past two days had been, she knew it had to end. Nothing final, but a girl needed some time to get her shit together. Besides she was never the type to be clingy. She dug through her purse and found her phone. She hadn't even turned it on since she'd left the club Saturday and today was Monday.

He walked over to her. "Slept good, dreamed of you."

"Wow, I'm the woman of your dreams," she said with a big smile, then powered on her phone. The iPhone came to life, with the voice mail and text alerts sounding.

"Somebody is looking for you. And missing you," Took said.

She scrolled through the phone, looking at her messages. "Yeah, my best friend, Unique is worried about me. This is totally out of my character—to just leave and not tell anybody—and be out of pocket for days."

"Well, then it's right for her to be worried then."

"Actually, it's crazy because her husband hit me up too." She smiled. "I know I'm in big trouble now."

"That nigga Kennard texted you?" Took asked.

"Yeah, but only because I'm sure Unique is worried."

"How long you two been friends?" he asked, fishing.

"We been friends for a long time. We met in prison and been besties since then. In fact, she moved here with me, and then met Kennard when she was out with me. So, I'm like her sister from another mister, and he's my brother-in-law," she said, proud to be a part of their family.

The man Tyeedah knew as Seymour nodded. "That's nice." He was glad that Tyeedah was a direct link to Unique. It was why he had targeted her. But after last night and looking at her smiling face now, Took felt a twinge of unease and found himself wishing that Tyeedah wasn't connected to Unique at all.

"I helped him pick out her engagement ring, helped him pick out the right place for her restaurant when he was trying to surprise her with his wedding gift."

Took shook off his discomfort. He couldn't be getting all soft now. He had a mission and he was going to see it through.

"So, where did he end up getting it?" he asked. "I heard it just opened up, but I haven't had a chance to make it by there yet."

Tyeedah loved how attentive Took was when she

spoke, especially about the people she cared about the most. She glanced at her phone, noticed the time and realized that she had been running her mouth for a minute now.

"We have to go," she said.

"Yes, we do, baby. There are a lot of things we have to go, do and see," he said. "So you want to call her and let her know that you alive?" He smiled.

"I will call her in a few. Just want to enjoy you now."

"I like the thought of that. Do you want me to order room service?" he asked, about to make plans to get their day started.

"Don't you have to go handle the business you came here for?" she asked.

He got up and took her into his arms. "You are the business I'm here for now," he said as sincerely as he knew how to say, which surprised him. *What the hell is wrong with me?* Took thought.

Tyeedah smiled because she really wished there was some truth to it. And little did she know, she was now a part of his plan.

She loved the feeling of being safe and cared for that she experienced being around him. "I definitely like that I'm a part of what you are here for now," she said, falling back into his hands. "But by no means do

I want to be that chick who stands in the way of a man going to handle his B-I."

"By no means would I let anything stand in my way of something that I need to do. But I hope one day to have a bond so strong with you that you take precedence over it all."

"I want that," Tyeedah said with a look in her eyes that let Took know that he was definitely putting down his mojo.

Then he said, "To answer your original question, yes, baby, I'm going to go out later and take care of it, but I want you back in my arms tonight. So, you go do what you have to do, and I will go do what I have to do and we will race back to beat each other back." Took had to take a step back himself. He knew he was good, but damn, he seemed to be either falling for his own game or her. And as he thought about it, long and hard, he realized it was the latter.

She searched his eyes for the bullshit and couldn't find any indication at all of the slop that lived there. "Okay, baby, that works for me. I want to be in your arms." And she hoped that the long French kiss convinced him of it.

Recovering from the embrace, he asked, "So, waffles? Pancakes?"

"How about chocolate? You?"

He smiled. "I'm yours anytime, anywhere," he said, "but what can I order you from room service?"

"I'm going to have to take a rain check. The race to return just started," she said. "Besides, you've given me plenty enough of 'room service' already."

MISSING

Two days had passed since the brawl had broken out at Kennard's birthday. Unique still had not heard a peep from Tyeedah, and she was simply worried sick. It was unusual for them not speak to one another at least a few times a day, so for Tyeedah to be completely MIA meant something was definitely wrong.

Unique had called, texted, and left messages on Tyeedah's voice mail, which was now full. Though she didn't like to show up to anybody's house unannounced, her only recourse now was to pop up on Tyeedah's doorstep.

She made the drive across the George Washington Bridge from New Jersey, through Manhattan, and to Brooklyn to make a surprise visit. As she parked, she hoped to, at the most, maybe find Tyeedah sick in bed. She rang the doorbell a few times before Tyeedah's younger brother, Lil-Bro, finally answered. It was barely opened when Unique pushed her way past him. "Where is Tyeedah?"

Lil-Bro looked confused. "Shit, I thought she was with you." He was in his boxers, yawning, rubbing his eyes with sleep stuck in the corners. "You know how y'all do," he said. "I just thought she was staying over at your house or maybe you two were on one of y'all girly trouble-making missions and shit." He raised an eyebrow.

Unique was en route to Tyeedah's room, but was stopped dead in her tracks by his words. "No, she hasn't been with me." She sucked her teeth, disappointed that Tyeedah wasn't there. "I haven't heard from her since the party."

"For real?" He questioned her in disbelief, and it was clear that he was beginning to get just as worried as she was. But he also knew his sister was a warrior. He thought again and said, "Man, she's okay."

Unique wasn't convinced. "Look, Lil-Bro, I don't think so. It's just so weird and out of character for her not to call me. Nor come home. I hate to think that something has happened. But she's never pulled anything like this before."

"But, if something had happened she would have called, or somebody would have by now."

Just then, the words "Baby, come back to bed" were heard before Unique turned and saw a big-booty light-skinned chick draped in a paisley-print comforter barely covering her backside grace her presence at the entryway of the living room near the hall. "Lil-Bro, who is she?" the girl asked when she noticed Unique in the middle of the living room, pacing the floor back and forth.

"Chill, this is my other sister." Unique could see from the expression on his face that Lil-Bro seemed to enjoy the woman's jealous tone.

"Nigga, you ain't got but one sister, Tyeedah." The chick picked up a pillow from the sofa and threw it at him while holding the front of the blanket with her other hand. "You must've forgot, I've been knowing your ass for a long time and we grew up in the same building." She frowned up her face. "So how come I've never met her?" she asked, as if Unique weren't there.

"Miss me with your bullshit," said a curt and callous Lil-Bro, "before I put your ass out."

Miss Paisley Print rolled her eyes and stood her ground, waiting for an explanation. She tried to act hard, but Unique could tell that Lil-Bro had hurt her feelings.

Unique spoke up. "No need to talk to her like that; the girl is simply asking you a valid question. Wouldn't you be asking the same question if you were at her house and some strange dude rolled up?"

Lil-Bro took in a deep breath, taking a second to decide if he wanted to explain himself. Finally, he said,

"This is Unique, man. My sister's best friend, and she's like a big sister to me. So don't even trip."

"Oh, sorry, baby," she said, contritely dropping her head and turning around, making her way to the bedroom. "Sister, I didn't mean to come off brash."

Unique cut her off before she could finish apologizing. "It's all good. Like he said, no need to trip." Then Unique turned her attention back to Tyeedah's brother. "Look, Lil-Bro, like I was saying, something just ain't right. I need you to get your ear to the street and see what's really hood, 'cause it sure ain't all good."

"Yeah, sure," he said.

"Okay, I'm going to put the bottom lock on the door," Unique said as she left, not knowing what else to do. Was Tyeedah locked up? Was she hurt, and needing some help? Was she dead? Only God knew at this time, because Unique surely didn't.

Back behind the wheel of her black Aston Martin, she was about to remove her phone from her Louis Vuitton purse to call Kennard when Beyoncé's "Run the World (Girls)" started playing. She'd always liked that song, but at that very second, the catchy tune had never sounded better. It was the answer to her prayers, because it was Tyeedah's ringtone.

Unique hurried to push the button to receive the call. "Oh *my God,* girl, are you okay?"

"Damn straight, I'm okay," Tyeedah said in a giddy voice.

Unique took a deep breath. "Thank you, *God*!" She was grateful to hear Tyeedah's voice, and then had to ask, "Well, bitch, where in the hell have you been? What in the world is going on?"

"Dayum, you sounding like you on some single black female shit," she joked with her friend.

"Bitch, fuck you!" Unique half joked. "I've been looking everywhere from heaven to hell for your ass for two days and I promise you I was a second from bringing in the CIA to help me out. Girl, I was scared and worried sick. I thought . . . well, I'm not even going to tell you what I thought."

"Girl, I'm good," Tyeedah reassured her. "I've been laid up, getting much needed good dick."

In a matter of seconds, Unique's worries changed from worry to anger to excitement for her friend. She knew that it had been a month of Sundays since Tyeedah had had any kind of sex, and she was well overdue to have her kitty fed.

"Give me all the details! I want details, details, details!" Unique demanded, as excited as she could be for someone.

"Well, girl, I met him at the party. And from the moment we laid eyes on each other, the attraction was ridiculous. For once, I went against my don't-fuck-on-the-first-night rule and I decided to just live in the moment and go with it."

"I ain't saying nothing; you know I've had my share of them in my single days."

"And you know how I feel about those one-night stands but like seriously . . . it resulted in the best two days of my life, girl," Tyeedah said, and Unique could feel all the smiles through the phone.

"Really? I'm so happy you had a good time. How did y'all leave it? And what do you think? And most important"—she paused, finally taking a breath—"what's his S.T.E.P. score?"

S.T.E.P. stood for Swag, Technique, Endurance, and Penis size—their personal grading system.

"Thirty," Tyeedah said, without even thinking.

"Dayummmmm," Unique said, impressed with this man because the scale usually stopped at ten, with one being the lowest. So this guy was quite something. "That's what I'm talking about."

Tyeedah was all giddy again. "Girl, I can't even make you understand how crazy good it was. The pillow talk was amazing and the sex was out of this world. He said he'd fucked a few chicks in his day, but only loved one girl in his life, but he has a connection with me like no other and it could definitely be the real deal holyfield."

Unique could hear the excitement in Tyeedah's voice. "That's fantastic, girly!"

"Yeah, but I'm no fool. I know it could go either way."

"Yeah, I know, but you are both grown, consenting adults, so you can work the fine print if you both want to."

"Yeah, but the odds of long-term relationships coming out of a one-night stand are slim to none. So, even if I never see him again, I will savor the two days we spent together and I'll never ever forget it—the connection— I felt with him. I really hope he felt it, too."

"Wow!" was all Unique could say for a moment, and then she paused. "Well, look at me and Kennard."

"That's different; you were created for each other."

"Who knows? You never know what God has in the cards for you." Unique tried to make her friend look at it in a positive way, then asked, "So, where is Mr. Good-Love now?"

"He went to handle some business and I'm running home now to shower and change, get pretty, and wait on his call."

"Girl, you are already pretty, so that's no extra work."

"Thanks, chica. He's supposed to link back up with me when he's finished handling his B-I. He said it wouldn't be too long, so I'm in a cab now, but traffic is real stupid right about now."

"Oh, okay, well, I wish we could've met and put in some face time," she said with a sigh, "but I know you're wrestling against time."

"I know, girl. Me too. I miss you, friend," Tyeedah said to Unique.

"Well, let me just give you the scoop real quick."

"Spill it, bitch. Hold on, let me guess," she said, before Unique could even speak. "Kennard bought you the new Bentley?"

"Girl, not even close."

"A bigger ring or maybe an island?" She made jokes because she knew that Kennard always showered Unique with the most extravagant gifts. "Share it, girl. Just spit it out."

"I saw Took at the party."

"You what? Saw who?" Tyeedah was surprised. "How did he get in? Are you sure it was him?"

"Yes! I'm positive it was him," Unique said to her friend. "And this can't be good"—she paused—"by any means."

"It's a big city with millions of people. Maybe he was here for something or someone else," Tyeedah said, trying to convince her friend, but Unique wasn't buying it.

"Girl, I know this guy inside and out. Being with him for the years as I was, I learned him like a dissertation. And I'm telling you, it was Took. And he's up to no good. Please believe it."

"Well, I know what you told me and I don't put nothing past these motherfuckers, but I think you might be overreacting a little."

Unique wanted Tyeedah to understand and normally she would have, but for some reason she wasn't getting it. Unique chalked it up to Tyeedah having love on the brain. "Well, girly, I'm happy you're okay. Stay in touch, please. Even when you're with Mr. Might-Be-Right, check in."

"I will."

"Well, make sure you do. I'm not going to dump on you. I gotta get to the restaurant anyway. Call me and let me know when he calls you and where y'all are going. As a matter of fact, if time permits, bring him by the restaurant so I can check this guy."

"I'll see."

"I understand if you lovebirds have other plans, but promise me, no more MIA shit."

"You got it, sis."

They hung up.

And within a matter of minutes, Tyeedah got a call from Seymour informing her that he had to go to Atlantic City to handle some business and then needed to make a stop in the city. He promised that as soon as both things were taken care of, he'd be all hers. She didn't ask, but she wondered what in the hell did Seymour have going on in Atlantic City?

WINNING AND LOSING

It was noon, when most hardworking people either were counting the minutes before lunch or already stuffing their face. The Borgata Casino, in Atlantic City, bustled with greedy gamblers. The absence of windows, which was a strategic part of most casinos, was intended to cause gamblers to lose track of time, while they lost their hard-earned money. All the while, bright lights and festive sounds, free alcohol and tawdry-dressed women and the ever omnipresent lure of that one big payday supplied enough stimuli to keep the betters wide awake and entertained, for days at a time.

Sitting at the blackjack table, Took peeked at the two cards and then asked the dealer for a hit.

The dealer's eyes met his and she did what she was told. Took smiled at her. She was fine: six feet tall without heels, skin the color of cinnamon and gray eyes. She slid the top card from the holder and flipped it over next to Took's hand.

An eight of spades, that gave Took a total of twenty-two, completely busting him out. The dealer said "Sorry," with her eyes, then with an accent sounding as if she may have been born on one of the islands somewhere in the Pacific. Fiji or maybe Tahiti.

"Me too," Took said, flashing a smile to let her know he harbored no ill will towards her and added, "But if we always won, it wouldn't be called gambling."

Took had never been big on gambling, but he respected the hustle of the casinos to the fullest. The casinos had their rackets and he definitely had *his*.

After downing what remained of his watered-down vodka and cranberry, Took said to the big guy sitting next to him, "Your luck seems to be even worse than mine."

In between hands, the two had been casually trading words for the past couple of hours.

"You win some and you lose some," Billy "the Grimm-Reaper" Jones said, shaking his head in disgust. He knew good and well that he was in deep shit. He was supposed to be in training camp. However, he had taken the money that Kennard had spotted him earlier that morning to hold him over until his big fight straight to the casino, thinking that he could flip the money and come up at the blackjack table. Besides a few hundred, he was back where he had started.

That's exactly what Took wanted to talk to Grimm Reaper about—winning and losing. After doing his homework, he found out that not only was Mr. Reaper in debt to the casinos and the IRS, he also owed 1.2 million dollars in unpaid child support to three different baby mommas. The six-million-dollar guaranteed purse for the upcoming fight was about two million short of what he even needed to get out of the red.

"Funny you should feel that way. I have been waiting all day to politick with you about just that."

Billy raised an eyebrow.

"Winning and losing," Took said with a warm smile.

"Haven't we met somewhere before?" Billy asked, his eyes filled with both curiosity and caution.

It was the opening Took had been hoping for. "Not really," he said, "but I was at Kennard's party—you probably remember my face from there. The name's Took."

They dabbed. The dude had mitts for hands. Took checked his Rolex for the time.

"You's a friend of Kennard's?" Billy inquired.

At the party, Took did ear hustle in on Billy and Kennard going back and forth for as long as he could without getting caught. But from what he did hear and gathered on his own—and besides the fact, Kennard had a substantial piece of money and time invested into Billy and his career—one other thing stood out . . . they didn't like each other.

Took chuckled a little at the question, shook his head and looked into Billy's eyes. "I probably wouldn't use the word friend."

Billy gave Took his full attention. "Well, what word would you use?"

"Adversary. I don't like him and I'm positive that he doesn't particularly care for me either. Another reason I want to talk to you."

"How about we grab something to eat to chop it up more in depth?"

Besides the comp food ticket in the restaurant, Billy didn't have much more to lose. Hell, it didn't cost anything to listen.

They found a booth inside of the restaurant near the back, giving them some privacy.

Took wasted no time beating around the bush. "I know a solid way to get you out of debt and stick it to Kennard all at the same time."

Billy had a surprised but an interested look on his face, so Took immediately said, "Hope the play wasn't too much, too fast."

Before Billy responded a waitress appeared. "My name is Dahlia. Do you know what you all will be having?"

Billy ordered two servings of salmon, fresh broccoli and a bottle of water. Took asked for the grilled shrimp, baked potato and a Heineken.

As Dahlia walked away with their orders, Billy asked, "What makes you think I want to stick it to Kennard?"

Took had expected him to be a little suspicious from the start. Billy continued, "We've gotten a lot of money together."

"You used to get money together—past tense."

"The man did get me a six million dollar pay day."

Took reminded him, "While he makes sixty million." Then to yeast it up more, he added two more cents, "Not including the twenty million he put on you to lose the fight." When he read the hurt all over Billy's face, Took couldn't resist adding more insult to injury. "All the while he was treating you like the hired help. Hell," Took added, going in for the kill, "I've seen him treat a valet with more respect than he does you."

The hook was in the water. Because the truth of the matter was that Kennard didn't respect Billy either.

Behind those suspicious eyes Took could see the gears turning. He was probably thinking about all those bill collectors hound-dogging him. "How much bread are we talking about?" Billy asked. There was the bite. "And what do you have in mind?"

Before the steroid scandal and assault charges in

the night club four years ago, Billy had been a heavy-weight champion of the world; literally, sitting on top of a fortune. Now he was pinching pennies and hoping that things worked out so that he could make it to training camp, since he had jerked off more of his advance money.

"For starters, I need you to throw the fight. And I want you to make a public announcement that Kennard blackmailed you into doing it. I want it to be so obvious that you took a dive that Stevie Wonder would be demanding his money back for the travesty."

"How exactly does that hurt Kennard, if he bets that I lose anyway?"

"Besides him being charged with blackmail and corruption, it would destroy his reputation as a boxing promoter, and may even bankrupt him." Took studied Billy's expressionless face. "Let him see what it feels like to be broke and left with nothing."

The thought of sending Kennard to the poorhouse made his dick hard. Took was sure that Unique would rather ride a dirt bike thru hell than stay with a broke nigga and this would be Kennard's and Unique's destiny, if Took had anything to do with it.

The two mapped out their plan and when it was all said and done, Took gave Billy some good-faith money and a first-class ticket to his training camp.

Took headed back to the city and couldn't help but feel like a man with the world at his feet. How could he not?

With his pawns in position, Took already had his opposition in check.

COUTURE CUISINE

Unique rolled up to the new and trendy Manhattan restaurant, Couture Cuisine, and while she was never one to brag or boast, she was proud to say that it was a wedding present from Kennard. The Upper East Side real estate had a reputation for being pricey— although when Unique asked Kennard, he wouldn't breathe a word of what it set him back. Unique was sure, she knew for a fact, that it had to cost upward of tens of millions.

Another $1.7 million was generously dropped to transform the four-story building into a dining oasis, including the basement, which was used as a mega wine cellar. The restaurant was by far the most expensive, not to mention the most thoughtful, gift she'd ever received in her life. And Unique loved every square foot of it.

Since the grand opening three months ago, she was always the first to arrive and more often than not the last to leave. Today was no exception.

Inside, a faint but distinctive mélange of scents wafted through the ventilated air. Unique inhaled, taking in what had become both a familiar and welcoming arena. It would be an hour, at least, before Robert, her trusted manager, and other staff started to show. This was the time she normally used to go over the previous day's numbers and the day's projections.

Project in the future and reflect on the present, she thought to herself.

Oftentimes, people spent so much time dwelling on their past that they wasted the gift of the present. Her mother, Brandy, was one of those people. Correction, the lady that pushed out and gave birth to her. Brandy was a lot of things—mostly a dope fiend and a punching bag or crack whore for some dope pusher—but in all the days that she walked the Earth was she ever a mother to Unique.

Just a couple of the reasons why, growing up, Unique learned to fend for herself with the two assets she knew she had: her body and her savvy, a brutal combo that got her through many hard times and tight situations—most of which she wished she could forget. But that wasn't reality and as much as she tried to escape her past, some things could never be forgiven or erased. She sighed and said out loud, "Such is life."

Exhaling, Unique made her way through the main first-floor dining room and passed the hand-carved mahogany bar that stood adjacent to her office door. The lock was disengaged—which was odd, she thought, because she never left her door unlocked unless she was actually inside. She was sure that Kennard wasn't there. He was the only other person that she trusted thus far to possess a key and she knew for certain he hadn't been anywhere in the vicinity.

Suddenly, it felt like someone was watching her. . . . She wanted to believe that it was just her imagination, that it was all in her head. Normally, she wasn't a paranoid type of person, but the feeling was too strong to ignore.

She jerked her head around, looking behind her. No one was there. Her eyes went from table and chairs to wall to wall. Then she felt silly. Why would someone be hiding inside the restaurant? Besides, she thought reassuringly, the alarm system they'd had installed was state of the art, so if anyone was inside she would have been alerted by the motion sensors.

After glancing up toward the second floor, definitely unsure of what she was expecting to see, Unique finally stepped into her office.

Immediately, Unique knew someone had been there. And if they were still around, she thought, as she brandished the nickel-plated nine-millimeter she kept in her purse, whoever it was, they were going to get more than they bargained for.

With her deadly piece in hand, like a surveillance camera she quickly surveyed the office. At the left of the entrance, the cream leather sofa set, where it always belonged, was two inches away from the mocha-colored accent wall. No room for anyone to hide there, unless Demi Moore was the intruder. The brief moment of levity brought a smile to her face, but it was short lived as she slowly stepped farther into the room. Reluctant to face what was ahead of her, she felt like a petrified person in one of those horror movies.

The desk was straight ahead; it had been a source of a lighthearted debate between her and Kennard at the time of purchase. He favored the more old-school traditional mahogany pieces, while Unique opted for a contemporary style. The tempered glass and chrome desk that she chose was not only sleek and fashionable; to her relief at that very moment, it provided a clear view to the back wall. Nothing was behind the desk but her ergonomic massage chair.

Which only left one place inside of her office where someone could be concealed. Unique turned to her right. With the fuck-you end of the nine leading the way, she crept to her personal shower-equipped powder room. Stopping at the closed door of the bathroom, Unique breathed in a lungful of air, her nerves dancing.

"I know you're in there," she said, facing the door.

"You can come out now and leave, or I can call the police."

Nothing at all but silence.

"I promise . . . you won't like your other options as much as the first two." The nine-millimeter was steady in her hand, and was trained on the door. At the slightest provocation, she would harbor no compunctions about busting a cap in a joker's ass.

Still, there was no sound or movement from the other side that she could detect. *Okay,* she thought. *If this is the way you want it, so be it.* Her left hand on the door handle, the nine firmly in her right, she twisted the knob.

To her relief, no deranged lunatic lunged out toward her. In fact, the bathroom was spotless. The open frosted-glass shower partition provided her a clear view inside the stall. It, too, was also empty. Maybe *she* was the only lunatic in the bathroom after all? She turned around, making her way back to her desk.

A quick glance at her Rolex watch confirmed that she still had a good forty-five minutes of alone time to go over sales and inventory.

Sitting down behind her desk she noticed it. It had been there the entire time, right on the monitor of her iMac computer, right where it would positively be seen. Someone had left a note.

I wasn't imagining at all that someone had been in my office, she thought.

The beginning of the message was innocent enough: CONGRATULATIONS ON YOUR NUPTIALS.

And then a second line, which chilled Unique's blood: COMEUPPANCE IS A BITCH! AND THEN YOU DIE!

With no idea how he had gotten into the restaurant, much less into her office, Unique knew exactly who left the intimidating message. *Fuck you, Took!* she thought to herself. *I will not let you get to me!*

Any illusions she might have had of Took's sudden appearance being a coincidence was now out of the window.

Immediately, she dialed Kennard, who said he was on his way.

While she waited on Kennard, she called Tyeedah and filled her in on everything that was going on.

Tyeedah couldn't believe it. "Seymour just called and said he was on the way back to his hotel from Atlantic City, and I was going to finish getting myself together and meet him, but under these circumstances I'm gonna head over to you."

"No, girl. I'll be okay." Unique wanted her friend there but at the same time, understood that Tyeedah should spend time with her new boo. "I'm good, and besides, Kennard will be here any minute now."

"And I'm sure he will come up with a sufficient way to deal with Took."

"Me too," Unique said, but she was still a bit shaken up.

Unique concluded the call the second Kennard walked in the door. He took her into his arms and she felt like she had found her refuge. "Baby, I told you that this nigga wasn't here by chance. And I know he came here for something, and knowing what I know about him, it's not to give us his best wishes. You don't know him like I know him. Baby, if you never took me seriously, then—"

He cut her off. "I do take you seriously, never think that I will underestimate any man and especially one who left you in Mexico and has the nerve to show up in my town."

"I know, baby," she said with a sigh, "but I can't stress enough to you, he's the most calculating person I ever met in my life, and if he's here and was at that party, he's here for a reason, and I'm sure he has some accomplices right under our noses."

"I doubt that."

"I'm telling you, babe," she said in a desperate plea for him to take her seriously. "I know how this guy works."

Kennard believed the words that were coming out of Unique's mouth, but had no idea just how treacherous this guy could be.

NO SURPRISES

Kennard wouldn't settle down until Unique agreed to have security with her and to take the next day off. The plan was that she would spend the first half of the morning at the spa and the rest of the day with Kennard. No work, only relaxation.

The spa was exactly what she needed, and she was blessed to be able to get in with Raphael at such short notice.

In order for the spa to accommodate her, she had to be the first person on Raphael's book.

When Unique arrived at the spa, she was so early that the receptionist had not arrived yet. She and Rambo, the big six-foot-seven, three hundred pound security guard, were greeted by Maggie, the owner of the spa.

"Hey, Mrs. DuVall." She always addressed Unique as the *Mrs.* now, since she had tied the knot.

Any other time, Unique would tell her to stop being so formal, but Unique loved the sound of her new last name. It made her feel important to know that she was not just anybody's wife, but Kennard's wife. Especially after all the drama with Fat Tee, this man had still married her. She not only loved everything about him, but she also loved the respect that came with her new last name.

"Hey, hon." Unique smiled, kissed her on the cheek. "Thanks so much for getting me in here. Girl, you have no idea, I so need this," she said. "Oh, and this is Rambo." She pointed to him as he grabbed a magazine and took a seat.

Maggie smiled, acknowledging Rambo and said to Unique, "No problem. You know anything I can do, I will. I just feel bad that Raphael isn't here yet. He just called and said he's running about twenty minutes behind schedule."

"No problem, I'm just grateful that he's on his way," Unique said, not disappointed that she had to wait. Raphael was well worth it. Though he didn't speak much English, his hands did all the talking. They were like butter and knew all the right pressure points.

"Well, I'm going to get you set up in a room."

"Perfect," Unique said with a smile.

Maggie was waiting for her after Unique got undressed and came out of the locker room. She led her to the peaceful, tranquil room where she would be serviced. She told her, "Make yourself comfortable and

Raphael should be here any minute. In the meantime I hate to run, but I have a facial I need to get started."

"Thanks," Unique said. "I'll talk to you later."

Unique lay on the bed, enjoying the moments of solace. Finally, the door opened and the masseuse walked in. *Not a second too soon,* Unique thought.

The soft jazz music the parlor used to relax its clients was soothing, but nothing put her in a better mood than a well-executed massage. Well, maybe a few things, but a pair of strong, well-trained hands were right at the top of the list.

Unique was already lying on her stomach, her face inside one of those padded, donut-shaped headrests. The masseuse removed the thick terry cloth towel from the back of her neck. Then he brushed on a generous amount of warm massage oil. Unique exhaled a sigh of relief in anticipation of the masseuse's touch.

However, out of nowhere the masseuse grabbed a handful of her hair and yanked her head back painfully. Before Unique could protest, his left hand came around and clamped over her mouth, holding her *and* her words where they were.

Unique panicked.

The hand on her mouth was too big and too strong to belong to Raphael. She tried to lift up, but the person holding her down was too strong.

The man assaulting her said, "It's me, bitch, and I

wish you would try to scream or act stupid." He spoke without malice as if he attacked women in the private rooms of upscale spas all the time. "Do you recognize my voice?" he asked.

Did she? How could she ever forget it? she thought.

She had heard the same voice in her dreams, every single night until she was finally able to fall asleep, in Mexico, where the owner of the voice had left her with no passport, to work off a debt in a whorehouse.

"Stop scrumming," he said firmly.

His voice wasn't a dream. It was real. All she could wonder was how in the hell did he get past Rambo and when the fuck would Rambo come through that door and put two to this nigga's head? She never really wished death on anybody, but right now, she wanted Took dead as a dead dick dog.

She did what he said, and stopped moving. She wondered what she could use in the room to kill him.

"I'm not going to rape you and beat you like Fat Tee did. No, I want you to feel something other than hard dick. I want you to feel hard times, bitch, and I'm going to make sure you do, or I'm going to die trying."

Unique had no idea what Took intended to do to her, but to say she was scared shitless was the understatement of the year. She knew him well and if she didn't know anything else, she knew he meant every word he said.

Still in a calm, cool and collected voice, he said, "I just want to deliver a message in person, so that there won't be any surprises."

What the fuck did he call this?

Then as quickly as he had appeared, she was free, the door opened again, closed and he was gone. The altercation had lasted less than five minutes and had almost caused Unique to piss her drawers. Then she remembered that she wasn't wearing any.

SPEAKING OF THE DEVIL

Since she had spoken to Unique last night on the jack, Tyeedah couldn't get the eerie words out of her mind. Regardless of how she tried to push them away, the same pieces from the conversation kept returning like an irritating itch. No. More like a nasty rash, she thought, that wouldn't go away.

You are not going to believe who I saw at the party.

In prison the two girls had built a strong bond. Once they'd lowered their guards and started to trust one another, Tyeedah and Unique shared everything, from conversation to camaraderie. The two dreamed big as they planned for the future while they also laughed and cried about the things they did pre-prison. Unique never really felt any kind of remorse or shame for any of the shiesty things that she had done in her past to the many men who she had stolen from or had manipulated. The only thing she wished would have turned out different was about the love of her early life, long before Kennard. She often carried on about how she had treated Took, one of her exes. She talked about the dude in such detail—the good times and how she fucked him over after he got knocked— Tyeedah had felt like she knew Took, even though she never actually met him.

Tyeedah gave the door, which she exited not even six hours ago, three quick raps. The door swung open before her arm made the short trip to her side. Seymour was shirtless, waves orbiting his head, wet from an apparent shower. "I hope you don't have company," she said jokingly.

With the casual dimpled smile that showed even, white teeth, Seymour pulled her into the room by the arm, and closed the door. "You know I have no company," he said, kissing her on the mouth and smearing her "Oh Baby" MAC tinted lipglass. "Until now." He grabbed her hands, looked into her eyes, and then kissed her on the forehead. "What's all this?" he asked, wanting to know what she had in all the rolling bags and tote bags she was carrying.

"It's your dinner," she said.

"Packed up like that?" he asked with a raised eyebrow, while trying to snoop in the bags.

"Get back, babe, let me get everything set up," she said as she started pulling out a tablecloth and covered the small table in the room. She set up the candles on it.

Took looked on, as she sat the containers of food on the table. "Where did you get food from?"

"I cooked it," she said with a smile.

"You cooked?" he said, surprised.

"Yes, I cooked for you, honey. I figured you been away from home and living out of a suitcase—eating out from restaurant to diner. I wondered when was the last time that you actually had a home-cooked meal. So, while you were out handling your business I decided that I'd prepare a real dinner for you."

Having a woman cook for him was nothing new. Most of the chicken heads he ran across couldn't boil an egg and the ones who could thought that if they cooked for him it was to the way to his pockets, and did it for points. However, he felt that Tyeedah went through all of this trouble because she genuinely wanted to for him, no strings or ulterior motives, only to make his life a little more comfortable.

Tyeedah was what he needed in his life. Time and time again, over the past few days she constantly showed it—that he needed her in his life.

"I would've invited you over for dinner, but with my lil brother there there's literally no privacy and I didn't know how you would feel about him being in our mix so soon."

Took didn't say anything because he was still digging the thought behind her unexpected gift.

"Anyways, like I said, I know you got to be tired of eating out."

"Thank you baby," he said and took her into his arms. "You make me so happy, and I want to work things out so that I can make you happy and that we could really be together—and build something. Real talk."

Took meant it, but knew that the odds of them really making it were slim to none. But she had him wondering how he could adjust his plan so that things could work out between the two of them. He couldn't help but wonder if Tyeedah had any idea that he was Took and that he was there to harm her best friend. He hated that he had fallen for Tyeedah and that he was now second guessing what he came there for—to make Unique's life a living hell. But if he went through with it, then he would most likely lose the one thing that he wanted to be his.

"Let me finish getting this set up for you. I know you gotta be hungry."

"It smells good."

He couldn't help but to think to himself, *Why she gotta be so right? So kind? So thorough? So sexy? So sexual? So considerate? Loyal? So everything I need and want? Why? Yo GOD, you got jokes. Your sense of humor is crazy!*

While she continued to set up the spread, he made his way back across the room to move his papers off of the desk where he had been sitting. But his butterfingers caused him to drop one of the folders and papers scattered across the floor. He couldn't get them all up quick enough, and she ran over to help him pick up the papers. Though Took tried to get them up fast, it was too late.

Tyeedah was shocked when she saw an old school picture of Unique wearing that red leather suit and some tall riding boots. It was the same photo that Unique had had when she was in jail. He also had the wedding photo of Unique and Kennard that had run in the newspaper.

Tyeedah wasn't dumb by a long shot. She knew what time it was.

She offered a silent prayer to God that her *new* friend, Seymour, wasn't Unique's *old* friend, Took.

But deep down inside, Tyeedah knew that God would probably wash his hands of this one. She probably wasn't going to be that lucky. Just when she thought that things might be finally falling in place for her with her love life, she had to be reminded that things are not always what they seem.

She took a deep breath. "I don't remember you saying who invited you to the party. Was it Kennard?" she asked.

Without hesitation or detectable deception, he answered, "Neither. Keeping it one hundred with you, because I truly fucks with you, baby, I purchased my invite off the Net and invited myself."

He stared into her eyes, as if he knew that the questions had only begun. Questions he didn't seem the slightest bit afraid to answer . . . but was she willing to ask and hear the real honest answers? Sometimes it felt better to accept a lie because the truth often hurt too much.

"How long have you known Unique?" she asked, straight to the point. "And please, don't lie to me."

He reached out for her hand; she pulled away, bracing herself for what she knew was going to most likely be some bullshit.

"Maybe you should have a seat," he said.

"Maybe you should answer the damn question," she responded, standing her ground and not wanting any of the fluff or the cow for the bull he was preparing for her.

Holding her glare with his own gaze, he said, "I've known Nique a while. The first time we had sex . . . she was sixteen and I was eighteen."

At that moment Tyeedah felt like rocks were grinding up in her stomach. The already small room started to close in on her. She sucked in a breath of stale air as artificial as their so-called chance meeting. "So why the fuck am I here?" she spazzed out on him. "Unique told me about that foul-ass shit you did to her about getting her out on that appeal bond, then taking her on the get-money spree and ultimately leaving her in Mexico. That was some foul ass shit."

"Hold on, baby," he said calmly.

"Hold on, my ass," she said. "You must think I'm crazy or some shit." She chuckled a bit and then asked, "So you thought that by you putting your hocus-pocus on me that you would seduce me into turning on my girl somehow. Yo, playboy, you got me fucked up. Ain't no dick that good that I would betray a friend, and especially Unique."

He listened to everything she had to say and now it was his turn to suck in a pocket of the sour air that filled the room. His lungs seemed to rock with it a lot better than hers. When he exhaled he said, "I had no idea you and Nique were as close as you are." With the casualness in which he referred to Unique's name, she couldn't believe she'd actually fucked this dude and had fallen for him. She knew there was an undeniable attraction but she still felt rotten.

"At first," he continued, "I thought I'd just met a pretty girl at an ex-girlfriend's party."

Tyeedah wasn't buying it, not even a little bit. "Who the hell do I look like to you? Suzy Sausagehead, huh? If you were keeping it so on the up and up then how come you didn't bother to tell me your *real* name?"

"I did tell you my *real* name. My mother named me Seymour. Took is my street name."

Tyeedah rolled her eyes. "Nigga, please. I don't believe in coincidence," she said, flipping. "There are no chance meetings or encounters."

"Well, I don't believe in coincidences, either, but," he added, "how come it's impossible to buy into the fact that maybe it was in the cards for us to hook up?"

"Easy," said Tyeedah. "Because you either stacked the deck or dealt from the bottom. That's why."

Took tossed his hands up, like the matter was hopeless.

She continued, "You could have given Denzel a run for his money with the acting. Yo, Unique was right about you. You got all your shit down pat, boy."

In his eyes, he wanted to explain it all to her and to make her feel comfortable. "What is it you want me to tell you?"

She shot back, "Try the truth, if that's even possible. I'm not even sure if the truth is even in you."

The thing that hurt Tyeedah the most was that she was genuinely feeling the dude—she thought they had chemistry—only to find out that she was more like his science project. She was likely a pawn in some Machiavellian scheme. She knew she should just put on her Air Jordans and take flight out of his life, but for some reason she just couldn't cut loose.

Took sounded contrite when he asked, "Where do you want me to start?"

Tyeedah remembered how skilled of a thespian Unique had said he was. "Why were you at the party on Saturday night?" she asked. "Start there."

Took looked upward and to the left, as if he were searching for the answer or a lie.

"That's a very good question," he finally said. "Actually I'm not completely sure why I was there."

"Is that all you got? You are not fucking sure?" One person could only take so much bullshit and she had maxed her limit. "I'm outta here."

Took pulled her back. "You asked for the truth. The truth doesn't always make sense—it just is what it is."

Tyeedah slapped his hand away. "Touch me one more time without my permission and I swear to God, I will cut your fucking hands off." It was a warning; not an empty threat.

Subconsciously, Took's hands, as if they had a mind of their own, sought refuge behind his back.

"Let me try to explain."

"Make it quick," she said, rolling her eyes with mixed emotions, but wanting to give him the benefit of the doubt.

"I heard Nique had come up. Married Kennard DuVall and living a fantasy life. Information came right out of the blue. And I didn't know how to feel about it," he said truthfully. "Mad. Jealous. Hate. Vindictive . . . or all of the above. I was like an emotion gumbo."

Tyeedah tried not to be moved by his sudden, so-called revelation; she stood expressionless and listened as Took continued.

"Sure. I contemplated several different ways I could make Nique's life a few rungs less glamorous. Unburying a couple secrets that dear hubby or the police might not know about. At the very least," Took said, coming clean, "I knew I could draw down a pretty penny, if I stayed quiet or not . . . and destroy her."

No emotions were intertwined with his words. He spoke as if he made these types of decisions every day. *No big deal* was written all over his face, but what was written in his heart was a whole other story.

"After I got here, I asked myself an honest question: Am I pissed at Nique because she found someone who made her happy? Or because I failed at doing so? Or am I just miserable and I hate that she is, despite the fact I left her to rot?"

"So," Tyeedah asked sarcastically, "how did you answer this philosophical question of yours?"

"I didn't have to," he said. "After I met you, my real reason for coming here changed. It seems like the more I was around you, I forgot about everything else."

"That sounds all peachy but at the same time, how can we be together?" she asked.

"I don't know. This may sound a little like bullshit, but please take my words at face value."

"What words are those?"

"Let me try to fix this with Unique. Let me try to make things right with her and maybe she will accept things between us."

"If I were you, I wouldn't bet your backwoods ranch on that one."

"Trust me," he said.

BIG TIME

Friday was the standing delivery day for the wine and liquor. Unique quickly learned that it didn't matter how well the food was prepared, how fabulous the décor, or how above satisfactory the service and waitstaff was: if the alcohol wasn't up to par—and in abundance—the restaurant wasn't worth the weight of its brick. It was a problem she needed to concern herself with because Couture Cuisine covered all of the above—this was why she had to be on point to get this liquor delivery.

This was the first time Unique had been inside the building alone since finding the note. She wasn't scared, however, because in a strange way she had come to enjoy that window of time before opening. She missed the solitude she had become accustomed to each morning and found solace in its peace.

Her thoughts were shattered by a sound from behind the bar. The noise startled her until she realized it was only the buzzer that was wired and connected to the service doorbell. The supplies were always delivered at the back door, to the basement, which opened out to the alley in back of the building.

He's here, she thought, making her way to accept the delivery. In the kitchen, Unique flipped on the light for the stairs and the entire sublevel below. It was 9:15 A.M. and like clockwork, the delivery was right on schedule.

Eighteen carpeted steps led to the wine cellar. Once at the bottom, Unique made a right, passed sixteen custom racks—each built to hold five hundred 0.75-liter wine bottles—before getting to the door that led to the huge storage room. The service entrance from the Second Avenue alley was ahead, to the left.

Buzzzzz. The deliveryman was laying on the button, the annoying sound bouncing off the concrete walls. "I pay by the bottle not by the minute. Have some patience," she spoke out as she reached the metal door. After disengaging multiple locks, she pulled the heavy door in on its hinges. "Where's the fire at, man?" she said as she opened the door.

The delivery driver wore the same outfit as he always did but hid his eyes behind some sunglasses. "Good morning," he said with a smile. Then he walloped her smack-dab on the side of the head.

His fist felt like a sledgehammer. The vicious blow caught Unique off guard and knocked her to the floor.

"I got yo fire, bitch!" Looking up from her backside, she was certain this wasn't the regular delivery guy. "I'm fitting to turn the heat way up," he said in a real Southern drawl.

Her first thought was that the fake delivery guy was Took, but the dude was way taller and had lighter skin than him. Maybe it was someone that Took had sent because he was famous for having other folks do his dirty work. If he was the same guy who had left the note, Unique knew she was in big trouble. She'd rather have faced a mugger only wanting the money. But this guy seemed as if what motivated him was personal. Then, like a theme from a movie, it came to her. The man in the blue uniform was Big Time.

She was outdone. The chickens had come home to roost. The past had caught up with her once again. Big Time pushed the door shut. "I betcha thought you would never lay eyes on me again."

Big Time was from Atlanta; he was an old cellie boyfriend. When Unique got out of prison, Big Time was one of the many vics that she and Took had paid a visit to. The last time she'd seen the dude, Took and a couple of friends had automatic weapons pointed at his head, relieving him of a shitload of drugs and money that he had stashed in his upscale downtown Atlanta condo.

Now, Big Time yanked her by the hair. "Kitty told

me to tell you that she missed that hot tongue of yours." The comment was meant to do exactly what it did—slap Unique in the face.

In prison, Big Time's girlfriend, Kitty, had everything legally an inmate could have, a myriad of things that weren't allowed inside. It didn't take long before Unique had turned Kitty's fish-smelling pussy lesbo. Back then, in Unique's mind, a girl had to do what a girl had to do to survive in the joint, just like in the streets—by any means necessary. Kitty was the first and the last bitch that she had ever given head to, let touch her, or given any other sexual favors for that matter.

A pair of handcuffs appeared from somewhere behind Big Time's back. He clamped them hard onto her wrists, so tight they almost cut off the blood circulation.

Not knowing what Big Time had brewing in his mind, too terrified to even think about it, Unique said, "I can pay back every penny. You don't have to do anything that you may regret later."

"Shut the fuck up, bitch," he said as he stuffed a handkerchief into her mouth and then pushed her up against the wall, face-first. "Any regrets that are to be had are going to be by you."

COMING CLEAN

Tyeedah finally fixed Took his plate and they ate in total silence. For the first time in his life, he really felt bad about his actions and he decided that he should just go ahead and lay the rest of his cards on the table.

So, he decided to break the silence. "I know some of the things I've done have really been fucked up, like I paid her a visit and threatened her."

"You did what?" Tyeedah raised her voice and could not believe what she was hearing.

"I didn't put my hands on her, but told her my intentions to make her go broke and lose everything." Before Tyeedah could respond, he said, "That's not what I want to do anymore. All I want now is to make peace and be with you." He sounded sincere.

"Is there anything else you haven't told me?" she asked.

"Besides me soliciting the help of one of Kennard's boxers to throw the fight and blame it all on Kennard?"

Tyeedah just looked at Took long and hard. She

was quiet. Even with all Unique had told her, she didn't know this guy could be so calculating. However, she seemed to respect him because he was coming clean. He had everything to lose but he still admitted to his treacherous plans.

Tyeedah was speechless and didn't know what to say for a few minutes.

He took her hand. "I apologize, baby, that you are in the middle of this, I promise this isn't how I planned or imagined that this would turn out."

She knew that, out of loyalty to her friend, she had to leave. But she couldn't leave, her heart wouldn't let her walk away as much as her mind told her to. She felt like her feet were cement blocks and emotionally she was chained to the room, to Took.

Finally, she spoke. "You say you want to be with me." She looked him in the eyes.

"And I do," he quickly countered.

She shook her head. "I'm not sure you are willing to pay the cost, it might just be easier to walk away and know we had a few amazing days but we can't ever be. We can chalk it up to that old saying—'It's better to have loved and lost than to never have loved at all.'"

"Baby, that's really not an option. I've fallen in the worst way for you—and willing to risk it all. So, share what's the cost?" He paused for a minute. "As much as my life revolves around money, I'd give it up for you." He tried to test the waters by kissing her on her forehead.

"I'm flattered that you'd give it all up for me. But real talk, nobody wants a broke-ass man," Tyeedah said.

Took cleaned it up quick. "Baby, I'm saying, I'd lose all for you right now, because I know I'd get it all back. I never had no problems making no money," he said confidently.

"Well, I have a thought."

"I'm all ears," Took told Tyeedah.

"I don't know how this is going to play out. I truly don't"—she threw up her hands—"but what I do know is for starters, to show an act of good faith, you have to tell the Grimm Reaper that he can't throw the fight and any money you already gave him, you have to count that as a loss."

"Done."

"I think you should let Kennard know what this clown was willing to do."

"I don't really want to make Grimm a casualty."

"Well, he was already a pawn anyway," she added.

Took nodded, not sure if it was a good idea, but he was willing to try for the sake of love.

"Now is there anything you can think of that might put Unique in danger or that could hurt her?"

Took thought long and hard, before he finally spoke. "Now that I think about it," he said, thinking hard, "there is something that I didn't really take heed of because I was on my own mission."

"What?" Tyeedah asked, gazing into Took's eyes.

"After I left the spa, I did a drive-by of Nique's restaurant, to try to map out my next move, and I noticed this nigga in the alley."

"It is New York City, it's not uncommon for dudes to be lurking in the alley."

"It was a nigga from the party. I thought I knew him from somewhere but I couldn't place him. I didn't put too much thought in that shit, and just assumed it to be someone's security."

Tyeedah listened patiently for Took to make his point.

"But now I think it was that nigga, Big Time, one of the vics that we got when we were on our robbing spree."

"Really? Are you sure?"

"Yes, I'm sure and I know that nigga ain't in the city to sightsee, he's up to revenge. In fact, he promised that he was going to hunt us down if it was the last thing he did."

"And he was in the alley behind the restaurant?" Tyeedah asked just to be sure.

"Yes," Took said with a nod. "I'm sure of it now."

Tyeedah reached for her phone and powered it on. She called Unique, but this time it was Unique who wasn't answering. Tyeedah got worried. "I need to put her up on her game, so she can be careful."

"Yeah, that's probably a good idea," Took co-signed.

When Unique still didn't answer, she called Kennard to see if he knew where Unique was. Kennard and Tyeedah talked for a few minutes before she hung up.

Tyeedah put her shoes back on and grabbed her purse.

"Where are you going?" Took asked, putting his shoes on too.

"Kennard said it was going to take him about forty minutes to get over to the restaurant. I can get there in twenty. She's not supposed to be over there by herself, but knowing her, she's probably in that restaurant alone trying to get some work done," Tyeedah paused for a second and let her mind run wild, "and God only knows." Worry was written all over her face.

FRIENDS AND FRENEMIES

What do you want from me?" she asked. "I told you that I could get you your money."

"And I told you that the only thing you running here today is yo mouth. I'm calling the shots, baby girl. Me. Big Time." He enunciated the B and T in his name so emphatically, spittle flew from his mouth.

Unique tried to keep calm and rational. "Then call the shot," she said in a composed voice. "Just tell me what it is that you want."

"I thought I'd made that clear in the note I had left on the computer, in your office. You did get it, right?" he asked. Then, not waiting for her to speak, he said, "To make your life feel like hell, before I kill you."

That's when Unique saw the gun in his hand.

Three shots rang out. Unique fell to the floor. At that exact same moment, Big Time, with slugs to the head and one through his back and out of his chest, died instantly.

Unique had passed out for a few moments. When she opened her eyes, she thought she was hallucinating. A pungent odor of gun smoke filled the basement's air as Tyeedah was asking, "Unique, chica, are you all right?"

"You saved my life?" she said.

Next to Tyeedah, with a smoking .45 in his hand, stood Took.

Big Time had forgotten to lock the service door when he pushed it closed. And the innocent, ultimately fatal mistake got him served up cold.

Thank God for her friends . . . and frenemies.

LET BYGONES BE BYGONES

After the effects to her eardrums subsided—the result of the explosion of Big Time's and Took's guns being fired inside and at close range, Unique heard the distinct sound of feet racing down the steps of the restaurant toward the basement.

Seconds later, Kennard and his right-hand man, Drop-Top, came crashing around the corner, with guns out and desperation in their eyes.

Once Kennard saw Unique lying on the floor, and Took standing over her holding a smoking gun, he snapped. Unique wouldn't have wished her worst enemy on the other side of Kennard's murderous glare. She knew that Drop-Top had the proclivity to kill without conscience, but she had never seen this side of her newlywed husband.

Both Drop-Top and Kennard took aim and were moving to squeeze their respective triggers. Unique screamed, "STOP!!! Took saved my life!"

Kennard didn't buy it and neither did Drop-Top.

The only thing that Kennard knew for sure was this was the dude that had stalked and threatened his wife, and tried to financially destroy him.

Even after knowing all this, he didn't shoot.

With his gun still trained on Took's dome, Drop-Top said, "Just give me the word, Kennard."

For the first time since entering the basement, Kennard noticed the dude stretched out on the floor with his boots knocked. Then he quickly scanned Unique's body for any sign of blood or injuries. There weren't any. All he could see were her pleading eyes.

"I know how it looks," she said. "But Took really did save my life."

Drop-Top gave Kennard a quick glance. No words were needed this time. If Kennard wanted the business done, he wouldn't have to get his hands dirty. All he had to do was nod and Took would be toast.

Kennard made up his mind. "Hold up." He decided to let the act play out a little longer.

Drop-Top wasn't happy with his friend's decision, but he would follow his lead. However, nothing short of an earthquake could make him lower the gun.

"For a man who says he's not going to do any harm, you sure have an odd way of showing it." Kennard was eyeing the gun still in Took's lowered hand as he spoke.

Took dropped the weapon. "My bad."

Kennard squatted down next to Unique. "Are you sure that you're okay?"

After Unique assured him that she was, Kennard gave her three kisses: one on the forehead, one on the nose, and the last one on the lips. He loved her so much.

Then he said to Took, "Convince me why you shouldn't already be dead."

Took cut his eyes over to Drop-Top, then he looked at Tyeedah, who was standing off to the side, looking worried. He knew she wanted to come to his side, but they both knew he was on his own for now with Kennard. He was either going to get himself out of this mess . . . or he wasn't. He turned back to Kennard.

"It's pretty hard to speak freely with a gun pointed to your head," he said.

"It's even harder to speak when you are dead," Kennard countered.

"Point taken." Took laid his cards on the table.

"Everything you thought of me, up until a few hours ago, is true," he said. "I came to New York to do you and Unique both harm. I don't hide that fact."

He had either bumped his head during the altercation or the boy had a death wish, Unique thought.

"But I didn't do it because of any hate towards either of you. My actions stemmed from the love I once had for Unique. I didn't want to see her happy, especially if I wasn't happy. But after meeting her," Took turned to

Tyeedah, "on a humble, everything started to change. I didn't mean to fall in love, it just happened."

Drop-Top sucked his teeth and said, "I hope you're not buying this Hallmark shit."

Took ignored the interruption. "The more my feelings for Tyeedah grew, the more I began to see what the two of you have. The simple version," said Took, "is that I was acting like a bitch that deserves whatever he gets. I won't beg for anything more, but I will give you my word, and my word is all that I have. If I make it out of this room alive . . . it would be as a friend and not an enemy."

Kennard gave his attention to Unique. "What is it that you want?"

Unique thought long and hard about the question. Took had threatened her life on multiple occasions, but he had also saved her life. "You and I have to talk," she finally said to Tyeedah. Then she turned to Kennard and said, "I believe him. To answer your question, I don't want him to die."

Tyeedah smiled with relief.

"Consider me sparing your life a wedding present," Kennard said to Took, "if the two of you get that far."

Tyeedah went over to Unique and gave her friend a hug. "I'm sorry and thank you all at the same time."

"We will talk it all out."

Out of nowhere, Drop-Top let one off into Took's

leg. Took yelled and fell to the ground, cursing and clutching his leg. "That's for leaving my sister-in-law in Mexico with no passport. That was some real bitch-ass shit."

Everyone stared in shock. No one had seen that coming, not even Took.

"I'll take that," he said as Tyeedah rushed to his side.

"Let's hope this chapter of your life is finally closed," Kennard said to Unique as he put his arm around her and kissed her on the forehead.

Read the entire *Unique* e-Novella series!

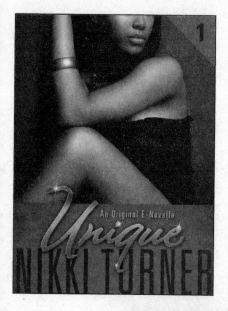

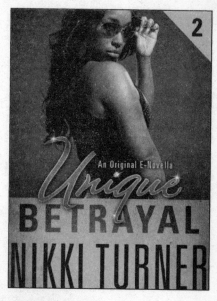

Don't miss these sequels from Nikki Turner!

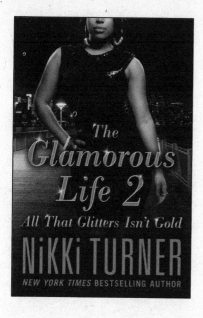
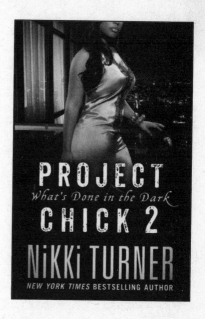

"Turner's raw writing makes for page-turning suspense...urban-fiction fans will crave this novel and all of Turner's titles."

—*Booklist* on
The Glamorous Life 2: All That Glitters Isn't Gold

"Nikki puts a new twist on an old favorite. As thought-provoking and witty as it is 'hood, *Project Chick II* is a great read."

—K'wan